HOLLYWOOD
A New York Love Story

MARC SÉGUIN

Translated by
Kathryn Gabinet-Kroo

EXILE
editions

Library and Archives Canada Cataloguing in Publication

Séguin, Marc, 1970-
[Hollywood. English]
Hollywood : a New York love story / Marc Séguin ;
Kathryn Gabinet-Kroo, translator.

Translation of: Hollywood.
ISBN 978-1-55096-397-7 (pbk.)

I. Gabinet-Kroo, Kathryn, 1953- II. Title.

PS8637.E476H6513 2014   C843'.6   C2014-900190-8

Translation Copyright © Exile Editions and Kathryn Gabinet-Kroo, 2014.
First published in French as *Hollywood* © 2012, Leméac Éditeur (Montréal, Canada)
All rights reserved.

Design and Composition by Mishi Uroboros
Typeset in Hoefler Text and Akzidenz Grotesk at the Moons of Jupiter Studios
Cover photograph by Claire McAdams
Back cover painting is a detail of "Astronaut No. 3" by Marc Séguin
Interior covers paintings are details of "Astronaut No. 1" by Marc Séguin

Published by Exile Editions Ltd ~ www.ExileEditions.com
144483 Southgate Road 14–GD, Holstein, Ontario, N0G 2A0
Printed and Bound in Canada in 2014 by Imprimerie Gauvin

We acknowledge the financial collaboration with the Department of Canadian
Heritage, through the National Translation Program for Book Publishing. We also
acknowledge the Canada Council for the Arts, the Government of Canada through
the Canada Book Fund (CBF), the Ontario Arts Council, and the Ontario Media
Development Corporation, for their financial assistance toward our publishing.

 Conseil des Arts du Canada   Canada Council for the Arts   Canadä

ONTARIO ARTS COUNCIL
CONSEIL DES ARTS DE L'ONTARIO
an Ontario government agency
un organisme du gouvernement de l'Ontario   Ontario
Ontario Media Development
Corporation

Canadian Sales: The Canadian Manda Group, 165 Dufferin Street,
Toronto ON M6K 3H6   www.mandagroup.com   416 516 0911

North American and international Distribution, and U.S. Sales:
Independent Publishers Group, 814 North Franklin Street,
Chicago IL 60610   www.ipgbook.com   toll free: 1 800 888 4741

HOLLYWOOD
A New York Love Story

"TENDERNESS
IS
LIKE
ALCOHOL,"

Branka had said as she cut a lock of hair, looking at herself sideways with her eyes fixed on the upper part of the mirror.

"What are you doing over there?" I'd asked before she could finish her sentence.

"I'm talking about tenderness."

She had looked at me in the mirror for a split second, cut another strand of hair and added, "I had gum in my mouth when I fell asleep. Now it's all stuck together."

"Were you drunk?"

"No, happy."

She used to pair a lot of words with tenderness: headache, moderation, drunkenness, respect, desire.

She usually stuck her gum on the headboard or on the wall next to the bed because she always forgot to throw it away before we made love. We'd kiss, then get into bed, no question of getting up to go over to the wastebasket. I never understood why she didn't just keep it in her mouth. It seemed simple enough to me.

I had kissed her back, almost directly behind her right ear, gently taking her swollen breasts in my hands. Milk leaked out if I squeezed too hard. She didn't say anything. I sniffed the nape of her neck, like a dog, nervously, as if it might be for the last time, to make sure I would remember.

December 24. End of the day. We were going to take a walk. Wanting to hurry her along, I'd said, "I'll wait for you outside." But I had stayed and watched her pull on over her leggings a dress that I had never seen before.

She had turned around, her enormous stomach stretched, deformed, in profile, and smiled as she squeezed her legs together and pressed a hand between her thighs. She said, "The semen's still seeping out" and rolled her eyes with the smile of someone who likes something that she should regret.

She had done nothing to stop it or to wipe it away or to change her clothes. I think she kissed my cheek. She touched up her makeup. "Do you think we can reinvent ourselves?" I hadn't answered, thinking she'd been speaking more to herself than to me. She tied back her hair and leaned closer to the mirror, tilting her head to one side and then the other, raised and lowered her chin, then let her hair down and carefully began again. Question of a millimetre, probably. I didn't say it: still too embarrassed. We'd known each other for such a short time. My sperm is running between your legs – the legs of a pregnant woman.

She was smiling. I was happy to know that there was still something of me inside of her. I had marked her the way a parish priest marks the forehead of a newborn on the baptismal font. Liquid is important in rituals. Wine at mass, water on the head, holy oil, extreme unction, "cheers" at a party, the exchange of saliva, blood from a wound or a pact or the kind that returns each month, sweat on the bed and proof of an orgasm. Mine: wanted, expected and honoured. Perhaps even a form of love. A superfluity. An intimacy that we will share with no more than a few people during a lifetime. Whether it be through conception or because she swallowed my semen, it was something magical every time and I never did understand it. A moment that can sometimes be abhorrent, during a rape for example, or sacred, when it is desired. She had said, "Thank you." Lowering her eyes, she added, "Not for that, but for all the rest."

The last time had seemed like the first time we'd slept together. She had said she liked it, having semen inside her, last April, when she'd gotten pregnant. A sort of pride or maybe a tear of happiness. I wouldn't even have ventured a guess. Never. Is the final result really worth all the effort made?

So unexpected. Branka.

An accelerated cycle of hours and years. Until now.

I
HAVEN'T
EXPERIENCED
WAR.

It's the contemporary drama of the white American male. It makes me less credible. Maybe even less free because I have never known subjugation.

I haven't experienced exile, I am not without a country, deported, tortured, an orphan, wretched or ruined. I do not have black skin in the midst of a white majority. I am not the lone survivor of a tribal genocide. I have never been in the same boat as the boat people. No one ever pulled me from the wreckage of a catastrophe. All I know of human nature is what books, television and everyday America chooses to celebrate and finance. When we confront a death, it seems like we're more alive for the others, especially if it involves violence or an injustice. There's a hypocritical, nervous respect in the shock wave that accompanies the tragedy. Concentric. A toy in a box of sugary breakfast cereal.

Branka Svetidrva was born in Sarajevo on March 20, 1980. That, too, made her beautiful. She heard the bombs. She inhaled the putrefaction of bodies and of ethnic ashes. She could have won prizes had she been a story in a movie or a book, the kind that stylishly bears witness to misfortune.

She spent the night of June 7, 1992 sleeping on the floor on her stomach, crushed by the sound of shells and the flashes of light, wondering if her apartment on the eighth and uppermost storey of a building in the heart of the city was going to collapse on top of her and her mother. They had always lived there. Sarajevo was a model of interethnic relations. Inter-religious, rather. Until then, enemies had managed to live peacefully together, on the face of it, their differences stifled and confined to secret thoughts expressed only to family and among friends. On a farm, you don't mix hogs with cattle. You can put a goat with horses and cats with cows, but never two roosters together or two bulls in the same paddock. A natural death follows. In animal husbandry, you can gather together each and every one of a single breed's females, but you can never put two males together. Because of war. Unless one is castrated. Made to submit. Otherwise, nature – quite simply established through this thing we call evolution – denies the right to coexistence. It simply cannot be. Submission is required for our survival. The Serbs, who were Christian Orthodox, didn't want the Croats, who were Catholic, to separate from them.

Running counter to the rest of the world, then, the Austrian-born German idiot who wanted to eliminate the Jews had been right about certain delicate facts of our condition; the problem was that he distorted simple observations and presented them as reasons. He had noticed natural strengths and weaknesses and had decided to make them fight to the death. Accurately illustrating what we truly are: efforts to survive. Vain and glorious.

"The mediocrity of dogmas," Branka had said when I asked if Slobodan Milošević was Hitler's first cousin. You can't build a skyscraper on ideas; at some point, it takes solid rock. The same goes for a country or a civilization. Blame it on the great ideas. Perhaps we too easily forget that we are conscious cells.

"The Declaration of the Rights of Man has just made me cynical and sexy," she had answered when I asked what she thought about it.

"Why sexy?"

"Because you're here today." Silence.

IN
SARAJEVO.
1992.

The kitchen in the bedroom and the bedroom in the kitchen. With the rooms thus reversed, it was harder for the rocket launchers to hit their target. Since April 5, the Serbs had been bombing the city. Hundreds of shells each day. Sometimes more than a thousand. Damage to property, but especially: "*Pazite*! Look out! Sniper!" Solitary wars, the ones with no numbers and figures. Led by militias with only one goal. In appearance, united. In reality, isolated.

Branka spent two months choosing to ignore the issues. On the morning of June 8, 1992, when there was silence once again, she got up and went to the balcony: from the street up to the fourth floor of the building where they lived, dust, ash, and the smoke from fires and explosions covered the city in a thick grey haze. Soft and cloudlike. As reassuring as a religion. "I got used to it." Minutes first. And then day after day.

The sun, the silence and the felt coverlet of suspended smoke, like in a plane, above the clouds. The most beautiful image she'd ever seen. She had just turned twelve. She would learn that beneath this protective layer there was death and solid proof of the damage we'd done. And that was the image she would create for herself. Through beauty. When you enter a mass grave through beauty, the dead bodies can become paintings by Goya and the stench, a perfume. "It was the discovery of a mass grave that put an end to the war, in 1995," she had said cynically.

She believed she was living in a world of certainties while it was on doubts that she leaned for support. And she would take all the support she could.

The Serbs played soccer with their enemies' heads. Bosnian heads. She told herself she'd probably do the same one day, if she ever had to wear a uniform. "My body is only an instrument that ticks off movements, symbolically, like a clock; it belongs to me but it has an end." That June morning, after a week of explosions, she had gone downstairs to the building's communal garden and planted pumpkin seeds in the earth. Never knowing if a little piece of metal would hit her, especially from behind, and break her in two. "This century is gushing blood." At twelve, she already understood this. You can cauterize it, suture it, inject it with heparin or watch it bleed itself dry.

Her generation would wear love as its bandage: "Will I be able to love someone one day, after all this?" she had asked herself a few weeks later, during her escape to France. She had read in a glossy American magazine that "courage is innate." But it was mostly the fear of dying without knowing whom she might love that had left her feeling so terribly romantic on that morning in June. Even at that age, she hoped she could one day love a man, despite the past few weeks, despite the soldiers who had entered her home at the end of August 1992.

It was also during that summer of war that she had her first period. A hot, sticky liquid running down between her thighs. It was through the actions that linked symbols to her conscience that Branka would stitch herself back together. Points of convergence first, in response to the most urgent needs. But it was with suturing thread that she finally created herself, that she repaired herself. Absorbable stitches. Him. Me.

"Not knowing if the sniper was going to shoot made me tough, cocky...secretly hoping that, if I did get shot, the sniper would have been kind enough to aim for my head. One day in early September, just before my escape, he fired twice, right next to me, and that was even worse. Shattered bits of earth and iron before the noise." She had known for a long time that the lone soldiers posted on the rooftops and in the church steeples were elite snipers. Snipers with real prowess.

She also heard gunshots in the distance. Ironically, hearing them was always a good sign. "I could even distinguish between a stray bullet and one that hit a body...by the dull sound it made when it hit flesh, and especially by the cries that followed the bang." The cries of others, the cries of witnesses. For snipers' victims, the metal bullet always precedes the noise. "It's like love," she would later tell herself. "It also comes tenths of a second ahead of what we've observed. Just enough of a delay."

I thought of her as lucky when she told these stories. Solemn and formal. I found her to be real. I liked to listen to her without flinching, as if it were perfectly normal, but more alive. One day, she sat on the bed and told me the allegory of Plato's Cave. About the acquisition of knowledge. She had completely changed the story, maybe a fundamental part of it remained, but all that followed had been transformed, transferred to the 21st century. Even though I knew the original, I preferred hers. Ever since *Casablanca*, I've hated all love stories. Because they are dishonest.

She never did harvest her three ripe pumpkins at the beginning of October because she fled Yugoslavia just before then, making it through the forest with the help of a network of accomplices purchased from a defense army as improvised as the other. Four days of walking and hiding to go

15

seven kilometres. And then a few hours to reach France and settle in with one of her mother's cousins in Paris.

She never would have harvested her three pumpkins anyway because one cold October morning, a sniper lying in wait in a church tower less than three hundred metres away had shot them to bits to amuse himself, those three dark-orange human heads.

When I was a kid growing up in the country, I also used a Crosman BB gun to shoot at Halloween pumpkins softened by the November frost, pretending that they were the monsters in *Ghostbusters*.

Our difference was found in details such as these.

I existed much more through her than through myself. It's a defect, like others have speech defects. But she never would have said it. I often wanted to tell her how much she had mattered. Perhaps she knew. We had talked about wishes a few weeks earlier. I assume that when you've lived through a war, you understand more things than other people do. Without always having to list them all.

And yet, she had already told me, it's quite the opposite. "The things you know the best undermine all the other things that are not absolute certainties."

We all fade from someone's view one day. When it hurts, I imagine it to be like pushing your eyes into your skull with your thumbs. The memory remains and starts to burn. It oozes. Then one day it coagulates and the first pain disappears. And then we remember having been able to see and that's when it really hurts.

She was never worried. She would have had a thousand reasons to be. The first being us. Me, in particular.

THE NIGHT
THAT SHE
GOT
PREGNANT.

She'd been talking for a few minutes and I wasn't listening. I assumed there were sounds but I wasn't sure of it. Each new time, I saw again all the other times when I wasn't listening. A survival instinct?

Why? I saw her lips moving and all the muscles of her face becoming animated. The eyebrows that arched when her mouth opened wide and frowned when she pursed her lips. She had said that she loved me four times. Four times in a row. We hadn't even kissed yet. It was our second date. "I just know, that's all." I could have assumed she was crazy. Or too quick to fall in love, like some others. I would have been wrong.

She had just told me the entire story of *Doctor Zhivago*. I could picture Julie Christie, Geraldine Chaplin and Omar Sharif. She had made a little fan out of cigarette paper as she spoke. Of all her Eastern habits, she had kept the one of rolling her own tobacco. She hadn't smoked for three weeks, but she still had papers and tobacco. I listened and said nothing. At the end of the story, when Zhivago dies, she had said, "My eyes must be sparkling."

I understood that she wanted to kiss me. Her lips were parted. Tunnel vision. "I won't be able to resist this urge for very long." She smiled. It wasn't a question. Not a request or an offer. We were sitting in a booth at a Jersey City diner and she had left her side to sit next to me and tell me four times that she loved me. The two of us were sitting on the same side of a booth for four. She had gone to the bathroom to vomit three times. "Nerves." And yet she seemed so calm. Contained. I thought it was the iodine in the sea urchins. "It comes from my father, according to my mother, I didn't know him, we're nervous and we don't know it until the entire contents of our stomach up and leaves...a genetic thing. I feel fine...it's just that everything I swallow has to come back up. So then I know I'm nervous, like I am now. Happy and nervous." Pause. She inhaled. Then exhaled. "I'm better now."

We took a yellow cab. Simple as that. We were going somewhere together. That was it.

She was strong exactly where I had weaknesses. She had given her address to the taxi driver. I had held her hand too tightly. She had gently held mine. She knew something that hadn't reached me yet.

And there I was, the one who only the week before I'd met her had still believed that I would always live waiting for love. Waiting is comfortable. It's the only place where I feel alive. In a state of expectation. Projected elsewhere.

YESTERDAY.
DECEMBER 24.
4:51 P.M.
JERSEY CITY.

She came out of the apartment after me. I watched her bolt the flimsy, piece-of-crap door, which I should have had reinforced, to this piece-of-shit public housing complex in Jersey City. We took the stairs because she preferred movement. She never took the elevator. "There's the stairway," she'd yelp, always happy when she spotted emergency exits. I opened the door and went ahead of her onto the first step of the entrance. My mother had done something right with me: not only do I consider women to be at least my equals, but in certain situations I return to my role as protector, like the man who walks on the street-side of the sidewalk or who goes down a stairway first, just in case. Branka was pregnant, almost at full term, so you never know. Her due date was December 27, three days hence.

The lobby was dark. Thousands of pieces of paper created a mosaic on the floor. JCPenney, Macy's, Walmart, Costco, Staples. Mailboxes with little glass openings above the numbered locks. A terrazzo floor. A fresh damp odour. Two doors made of glass and dull aluminum. I held the door open with my foot and waited for her to exit. Then me. Hands in my pockets. Hands in my pockets. Hands in my pockets. Branka brushed by me and went out first.

It was from behind that I saw her alive for the last time.

It was December 24, 2009. 4:52 p.m. That is what would appear on the police report. Outside, the snow, freshly piled up. Shovelled whenever necessary. Adults who rarely see snow turn it into a neurosis. They spread salt as soon as a low-pressure system is forecast, before the snow even falls. A lot of snowflakes for this state, which is accustomed to the sad, dry, pale-green winters of the East Coast. The light cast by the streetlamps was strangely white for the city. It was evening.

Corner of Montgomery and Florence Street, in New Jersey. In front of a park with its children's play area hunkered down for the winter.

I saw her wool hat move before I heard the sound. I don't know if I heard the sound. My ears were ringing, my whole head pulsating. The sound of a malfunctioning receiver. Stuck between two stations. A mistake. To me it seemed like the sound of a rubber band snapping. Two hundred decibels in a single sound. A single noise. But I'm not sure. I'm missing a fraction of a second. I must have blinked.

She fell, propelled forward. Separated from her consciousness. The grace that gives the appearance of life was no longer present. The sound of her head violently hitting the sidewalk. Or so it seemed, because my ears were paralyzed. And all the blood running out more slowly than I would have imagined. Slow and liquid.

How could such a tiny hole have done so much damage? An awkward excuse. Coagulated. In the middle of an ellipse, the end. An ending. Particularly for her.

The preliminary investigation would conclude that it had been a stray bullet. I would have liked it better if her head had been split open by a meteor one August night. Killed by the Perseids. It would have made me believe in something bigger, but that wasn't the case.

Jersey City is the deadliest city in the eastern United States. Perfectly normal for bullets to wander aimlessly. I've always thought that events that progress in a straight line are inevitably truer than those that zigzag. Christmas Eve, 2009. Branka was twenty-nine years old.

AFTER
BRANKA DIED,
I
WALKED

all night long, from New Jersey to Brooklyn, in twenty centimetres of wet snow, with no concern for the slush puddles beneath. Sometimes the water came up to my ankles. I followed the thousands of steps already tramped into the snow on the sidewalks and intersections. Walking, like the sole proof of intelligence. Moving forward. To thwart the sirens and the internal alarms. I believed that all those boot-prints and shoe-prints knew where they were going, but the truth was that those tracks only knew where their steps had already taken them. For the most part, they led up to a television or into a bed. Good and docile consumers. Silent. We're told what to eat, how to dress and even what to think. All of it under the auspices of gratuitousness, favours, normality and entertainment. The choice is simple. We no longer improvise.

I promised myself, among other things, to refuse love in all its forms. All, even the most sincere. That was just before the booze. No anger or stages of mourning with denial and disbelief. No more phases constructed by psychologists or philosophers who've had no experience and had to learn everything from their books. Nothing could have helped me. Just completely drained. In one fell swoop. Used up.

I don't know how I managed to be in love. It was nothing less than a miracle because that's what I would have distrusted the most. Especially tenderness, and specifically, the effect it has over the years of lowering inhibitions. A smile, a glance, a gesture, a hand, a touch.

Branka always cried on a single lungful of air. She held her breath and then the sobs came out. Tumbled out, rather. Forced. Like the air that we violently inhale after spending ninety seconds underwater. Tears. A flood of words. And silences. Time to recharge her batteries.

In the best-case scenario, I would spend several years learning, or accepting, that tears can flow for reasons other than pain. When it happens outside that circumstance, I find it a problem. She sometimes cried when we were making love. At first I was scared. It's usually a good idea to help people who are crying. Even when they have a pocket of happiness in the middle of their body. I thought that water coming from your eyes was like the little red thingy that sets off the fire alarm in public places. You touch it only in absolute emergencies to summon the firemen. No false alarms. My mother taught me that you cry only when you're not okay. Not for nothing, and especially not from happiness. The association had been made. The ignorance of great sentiments.

I vow not to be in love anymore. Just a little sadness for the fifty years I have left, technically, to live. Without any cynicism. Not my nature, perhaps, but the one I impose on myself. Not even a decision, it's become a feeling that I believe in. That will survive for a few years.

Branka: "I'm disgusted by the life expectancy statistics because they lie. People never lie to do harm; they lie because they're trying to protect themselves from the truth. Or to hypocritically get closer to it."

She was there, between the times when she said, "I feel ugly" and I replied, "You're beautiful." Right there. She declared that she loved me, with an overabundance in the words, because I was like a child in an adult life. "When a man lowers his head as he's shaking the hand of a woman he's meeting for the first time, it means that he's very attracted to her and is available." Smoke signals. Red.

She won't say anything ever again. Collapsed, heavy with that belly made huge by the child inside, on that sidewalk like when Zhivago dies, face down, in another century. With my semen still inside her. She had been in the crosshairs of a firearm's power scope several times before, she had avoided so many bullets fired by lone snipers, destined to kill for their war of faith, and here she is, felled by a stray bullet in a country at peace. I see no irony in it at all. Not even the most idiotic of coincidences. That's just the way it is. That'll teach me to love someone who loves me back.

I would have liked to lift her head from behind and push it against my mouth, kiss her one more time, savage and tender. A forced kiss, stronger, a bit foolish.

Do you think it's true, Branka, that once we have nothing left to tell, we die?

Everyone reads his own book, even if it's the same title for all of us. It's the "mask" game: everyone thinks he's more cunning than the next guy. That is how some people get cheated, others get rich or an invisible contract was signed. I'm lying to all of you and I believe that you don't know it. And you say nothing. We accept it. That's the first rule of the game. The mask is often as, if not *more* interesting than the true face of daily life. I guess that's why theatre and fiction exist. Beyond the self. Beyond us.

Everyone is convinced that O. J. Simpson killed his wife and her lover. But he got away with murder and no one worries about it anymore. Because there wasn't enough evidence. With a dull knife, no less. Amateurish butchery. Every individual reads his book and wants to believe in it. The jury believed it. It all comes down to the evidence. There are little truths like little justices. I use the great Justices, in accordance with protocol, to make me smile on the days when I am sad.

Naturally I was an important witness. The neighbours knew me. There was a lot of blood. I don't know why I didn't immediately think of *Kamouraska*, with all that red on the snow. Anne Hébert, Boris Pasternak. Galloping horses, a sleigh on a snow-covered road, a blizzard, a man bleeding like a stuck pig or with a wound in his gut, tracing kilometres of his blood across the white winter. It escapes. It goes nowhere. Its flight is internal. When you bleed to die from within, you never go far in history, unless you're an important victim. Then you can become a memory or a phantom around which a few orbits will be made. Like the moon.

Maybe I didn't think about it because this was a woman I loved. Reality often escapes me. More often than it should. Just for her, I would have lost weight or gotten a rare disease; just for her, I would have donated my marrow or used all my strength to go into remission. I know that now.

When the shot was fired, in that very instant, I knew what actions to take, instinctually, a thousand-piece puzzle completed in ninety seconds. We think that we're staying in place but we move on a vertical axis. We languish on the same terrestrial coordinates of latitude and longitude but we soar higher and farther than the black sky. X, Y, Z.

Branka in June: "Death lulls us and attacks us with its culture. And it is ingenious." I hadn't answered. Had she been reading out loud? We were stretched out on the bed. She thought I was asleep.

The streets were hastily plowed. The sidewalks were still white. I checked: the stop lights kept working even when there was no one at the intersections. With the same constancy as great ideas and the tides. I checked that, too.

You're dead, Branka. I still have blood, your blood, in the form of a U at the end of each finger. It dried where the skin meets the nail. It's sticky at first. Then it cracks and flakes off. Even after several washings with hot water in a white Gerber sink, the U-shapes are still there. What does it mean, the U? Am I supposed to find a word that starts with U or is it like a Scrabble game where everything that goes with the letter can earn you points? Everything is moving fast. I should stop.

"Some anchors never reach the bottom of anything. Or then it will be too late." Branka, also in June. She sang in French with the accent of a cabaret singer from the 1960s.

Yesterday. Sidewalk. She's dead. She was smiling and I was afraid. It's always suspicious, someone smiling to himself. When I turned her over, I swear she had a smile on her face. She was suspended over her balloon of a stomach. A smile like the one you have after making love. Soothed. The eyes would be of no further use. A moment.

I pulled her hat off. A navy-blue hat bearing the New York Yankees' initials. It was my hat. A hole. I kept it in my pocket. The blood was still sticky.

Was that a smile or was it pain? You shouldn't do that. I stopped looking. Eyes open. I kissed her, me with my eyes closed, on her cold nose. I pulled on her silver chain from which a cross hung. It easily gave way. It's always the clasp that breaks.

The mystery of being two. The mysterious mystery of having been two. You've never really met someone until you've had expectations together. At the same time. Or hopes. After that, it's a risk. And that limits the likelihood of having several true friends. Because true friends are like frozen apples on a tree in winter, there are so few, they fall. It works out well, in spite of us.

A fraction of a second. Like a black hole. Not a void but its polar opposite. A density of all that can exist at one time.

What were you thinking about?

Did you have time to realize that it was over?

You would have nodded your head.

Did you have time to feel pain on the sidewalk where you fell? Or was it as comfortable as a pillow? I like the idea of eiderdown.

The mystery of being two. I acted fast. Where the blood had touched the snow, it had melted it a bit before coagulating. A slight depression like when you pee on the bare ice of a pond in December. And like when you put maple taffy on the snow in March.

I stood up and left when the sirens appeared. Sound can appear the same way lights do. Hands still in my pockets, first walking rapidly and then at an ordinary pace. Disappearing like a generic man. Behaviour conforming to society's expectations. Normal speed. Everyone I met must have thought that I had the same rhythm as them. Another anonymous man, like the billions of stones erected in cemeteries that we have for centuries reduced to nothing more than two dates. Inside bloodied and torn, the façade intact.

The police report will say that there must have been someone with her when she was killed because the baby, found alive, had been delivered from her belly before the ambulance drivers arrived.

BRANKA
AND I,
WE WERE
NEVER

really a couple like those who like to broadcast their status. We'd known each other only a few weeks when she told me she was pregnant.

"Was it me?" I'd asked.

"Well, it wasn't the Holy Spirit," she had stated simply.

She had been born a Catholic, which is often reason enough to be at war. In America, we often forget the impact a religious state has because we are anesthetized by our diversions.

She was a constant reminder. Yes, yes, I repeated over and over to make myself believe it a bit more: we come from a world built and torn apart by beliefs. We forget that. Especially here in the United States, where we have the luxury of being able to think about things, rich and educated. Young countries don't have a memory yet. That comes later in history. For now, America is like a spoiled child. Naively so.

I like the idea of the Holy Spirit. A surveillance camera with undeniable power. "If everything goes as planned, the 21st century will not be religious, it will be chemical. A very long pause in Christian mythology. And even with tons of makeup, we'll still see the wrinkles." Branka loved raisin bread; she'd eaten it the entire time I'd known her. "A luxury when there's a war and you're poor. Have you ever been truly hungry?" she had asked.

Everything is possible. I know that now.

April 2009. Branka and me.

We had met at Easter, in Montreal, at a party to celebrate the engagement of mutual friends. She knew the girl – a Croat who was studying at McGill – and I knew the guy – one of my colleagues from university. I was standing and talking, or listening rather, to someone. My strong suit is listening. Especially remembering. I rarely speak and that impresses people. It gives me a certain power. The benefit of the doubt. I don't utter a word for several minutes and people look at me weirdly because I don't comment on their boring nonsense about work, projects, restaurants, music, family, or Oscar night. I prefer to talk about the weather when you have to say something.

She appeared quite directly, without premeditation. A simple smile. Her eyes. A sudden desire. Intelligent. Sincere. A rare experience for a man.

She had simply said "Branka" as she held out her hand.

She was breathing quickly. Out of breath. After a few long seconds, she said, "I get palpitations from my nicotine patch." She had been trying to stop smoking for several weeks.

We do not choose our attractions. We do not choose our attractions. Do we say it often enough? They come to us through a force all their own. We do not choose our attractions.

She had been attracted. Me too. As much by the head as below the belt. I hadn't understood anything at first. We make up an idea of what we want, what we like, and then suddenly the idea we created is nothing more than a little pile of fragile, weightless dust. I had pictured her tall, strong, serious, shoulders thrown back and head held high, with red hair, thin fingers, pale skin and bright, feline eyes. She turned out to be of medium height, a brunette with a bit of a tan, a long neck, and big dark eyes. And she was smiling. When she listened, you could see her top teeth, her mouth left slightly open.

Beauty is found in the details. The tiniest of details.

Truth and common sense do not always stand at the pulpits of churches, synagogues and mosques. Fortunately. This was true of that spring day when I met Branka for the first time, on Good Friday, April 2.

From that time on, I believed I was attached. Even if I had ten more years. I was also going to get married one day, start a family, buy a house, a cottage in the country. A proper life, not yet entirely laid out but on a path that had already been cleared. And I was going to do what generations of immigrants had done in a new country: distance myself and my family from all the effort to survive through years of sacrifice and hard labour, in the name of the children's future.

Signs of comfort. When she was tired, especially when she woke up in the morning, she was cynical. "Life is usually simplified by social expectations that are easily predicted and fulfilled. They ask us to be a couple, to live together and have a mortgage, a dog and a car. And projects. From the time we're little children, they instill us with illusions, especially in fairy tales, using a plot that we stick to, like incompetent accomplices, even though we haven't the faintest clue about its meaning. We work all week and buy stuff on the weekend. To improve ourselves. Evolution doesn't think ahead; it's just there, sitting immobile, in a mall parking lot. Or posted on a business' awning. Or like the Big Bang, during store business hours, expanding."

Then things happen.

THE
GUNSHOT.
THERE HADN'T BEEN
ANY ECHO.

Muffled by the snow and dampness, absorbed like the blood. Even before her head hit the ground, I knew I would be needing my Swiss Army knife. She was bleeding so heavily. It leaked out slowly but there were litres of it, accumulating in a glistening opaque puddle. I was impressed by how much there was. I had turned her over onto her back. I glanced around: no one, no noise. Cars in the distance, it was pitch dark. Only the sounds I was making. A kiss on her nose. I thought I heard a dog bark. I opened her suede coat, which she had found in a second-hand clothing store. I violently raised her dress and pulled her stretchy leggings as far down as I could. I cut from left to right – I'm right-handed – without paying too much attention to the line. I pressed very hard at first, to break the skin. The rest proceeded of its own accord. It still bled a fair amount. I was careful not to push too hard on the little stainless steel blade so as not to injure him.

Him. I pulled very hard on his shoulders with one hand while holding his head, from the front. Through the rising vapour. It was burning hot. I pinched the cord with one of Branka's bobby pins, bending the metal into a loop. I cut. It took a few seconds for him to cry; he was blue at first and then became red, sticky, covered with a layer of protective mucus. He opened his eyes and cried. He turned pink within a few seconds, from the oxygen filling his lungs. Life might actually be located in the middle of the chest and not in the head. I had cut the cord and said, "Hello! Welcome, my little man, and Merry Christmas." I cut the straps of Branka's dress and put the baby on her warm, full breasts. I closed her coat and hastily buttoned it up. Sirens at the corner of the street. Someone must have called 911. I stood up, turned my back and walked away, quickly at first, without ever looking back. Then at a normal, blameless pace.

The newspapers reported that there had been a single gunshot. And two ambulances. Branka had died.

The baby had survived.

I MADE
IT
ALL THE
WAY

to Brooklyn. Two rivers between us. I stopped for a moment on the bridge over the East River. Lights reflected on the waves. Hypnotic. It was dark but I could see that the river flowed southward. Toward the ocean. The water's current calmed me. There are people who throw themselves off bridges. Never understood it.

And I walked some more, to solid ground. I went into the Deli Store at the corner of Scholes and Graham. On all the television screens that I'd seen on my trek from New Jersey, even the giant one in Times Square, and on the Manhattan radio stations and the ones here, probably everywhere in the world, they were still talking solely about this man orbiting around the Earth. History's first space terrorist, they said. Playing in a loop were images of a man putting on his helmet as he walked and a close-up of the Chechen flag embroidered on his shoulder. Images of him entering a rocket's airlock. Voices. Predictions, diagrams of orbits. A frenzied broadcast. Strobo-scopic. The astronaut was going to die in a few hours. Breaking news.

I looked at the Deli Store's rack of newspapers as if what had happened to Branka could already have made its way there. Her death, however, would be eclipsed by someone else's, a more spectacular one.

Two men came in behind me as I was looking at the cold meats in a refrigerated showcase. One of them yelled a few centimetres from my ear: "I hate winter 'cause there ain't no fucking baseball and I love fat butts." The clerk politely said,

"Sir, I'm sorry, but I have a customer here," meaning me and wanting that to keep him quiet. The guy who'd yelled simply replied, "Doesn't matter that you have a customer, I still love fat butts."

"Turkey breast," I said when the clerk looked back at me, raising his eyes and shoulders in unison. An Indian-Pakistani-Sri-Lankan-Tamil clerk like thousands of others who have asked me what kind of sandwich I wanted. In the world I live in, I meet Indian-Pakistani-Sri-Lankan-Tamils only in corner stores or when they're driving a taxi. And they're always men. "Yes, turkey." It was Christmas after all and where I come from, you eat turkey on Christmas. "Yes, on a roll." I must have looked like I was starving. "Yes, with everything, lettuce, tomato...yes, of course, American cheese." I paid. He backed away, sat on a stool and stared at the television behind me, which was perched on top of the refrigerator containing milk, beer, Gatorade and Vitamin Water.

What is it you believe in, you who comes from a country that is twenty hours ahead of this one? How do you feel on the night when people celebrate the birth of a man you don't give a damn about? Do you also buy billions of useless gifts?

Do you know how to love in your beautiful countries that are so warm, so chaotic and so far away? Do you tell yourselves the truth or do you also have an industry of lies covering everything up?

The sandwich tasted of curry. Or cumin, in particular. I could never remember the five spices that make up curry. He spoke not one word when, as I handed him the money, I told him that the woman I loved had just died, a few hours earlier. I don't remember if I spoke in English or in French. My feet were soaked. And there I was, eating a turkey sandwich. They add curry to America's white, sweetened, factory-made mayonnaise. He answered me, smiling awkwardly – that's what they show immigrants in this lovely country – saying that I was entitled to a free can of Coke. I took the Coke. The red matched the red around my fingernails, or maybe it was a little lighter. My fingers still smelled of the baby. Not the smell of clean, perfumed diapers and talc. The smell of the womb.

HOW DOES
IT WORK?
TAKE A SHOWER?
A BATH?

How does distance settle in?
Branka?

Branka used to clamber up every church she came upon since she was a child. Not very high, but she tried every time. She'd go along the walls for a few metres and then climb back down. At first I was embarrassed. Four or five months later, even with her swollen stomach, she kept it up and it made me smile. One church, one climb. Simple. I was jealous. She loved the buildings and the architecture. She rejected the interior.

I thought that all pregnant women liked it when people touched the baby through their belly. Not Branka. Tenderly. It was hers because it lay within her heart, like a fantasy or a thought. You don't touch prayers.

I began to love her the day when she held my gaze for a long time. That was in May. She was five weeks pregnant and I had told her that her breasts were heavier. "Your breasts have gotten bigger." She smiled and looked at me for several seconds.

I
HAVE
A
SON.

From now on, I will be free to be a slave to my own subjugation because I myself brought him into the world. Delivered.

"Did you really think that love would be some sort of spell that's cast so that some other person can profit from your loss of self?" We were walking around the Upper East Side in late spring, looking for a crib for the baby. I had been wondering up to what point we can upset the established order of things when we change some of the data, about another person's right to live or die.

"All men are created equal. Maybe. But there is so much inequality in how men live and die." She had sighed and shaken her head through the city's noise, as we walked by the United Nations building. Without even looking. "It's a magnificent building, but they forgot to put up bell towers." Still without looking.

There are always sirens in New York. From Brooklyn to the Bronx, from Harlem to the Statue of Liberty, there's always a police car responding to a distress call. At every hour and every minute of the day or night. It's hard not to feel guilty when speeding cars wail at the social present twenty-four hours a day.

After swallowing my sandwich, I went into a Wine & Liquors. I had taken off my cap. I picked up a bottle of Jameson because I have some Irish blood. In Ireland, you are obliged to remove your hat upon entering a pub or bar. Otherwise you get beaten up.

For the first distancing, I chose alcohol.

And then I lost track of the time. I woke up in what looked like a makeshift dwelling. Very dark, a former auto repair shop, now abandoned. What had once been a parking area was now a junkyard. I was daydreaming, confused, about Branka's full belly. The door was insulated with old newspapers that you could see from the inside through the cracks in the boards. The roof, which must have leaked, was stitched together with scraps of sheet metal, asphalt shingles, tar and worthless pieces of wood. A home as well.

SARAH
AND
HENRY.

They had been a couple since 1961. Through crises, wars and fashions, time had taken its normal toll on them. It had been a long time since they had loved each other the way they do on posters, but they loved each other in real life. The life you live, not the one you avoid by going to mass or watching TV. They had turned their backs on their society. They lived on nothing. They didn't love each other with greater happiness because they decided to avoid the laws of consumption, but because they believed in it together. As a couple. Bonded to one another.

Heat salvaged from the dryers of a neighbouring laundromat warmed the room. Water came from summer rains or condensation from the air conditioners one building over. Light came from the sky through fiberglass panels or from a candle whenever they found one. The walls were made of grey cinder blocks. An old Clairtone television was their only contact with modernity. Hooked up to the glowing *Emergency* box of the old emergency exit sign. The only channel with good reception was ABC. At first I thought it was the radio because of the voice, but it was actually a TV whose screen no longer displayed an image. Just the audio. A TV for the blind.

They were airing, in a continuous loop, the exalted narration of a catastrophe: a special program about this Russian astronaut, Stanislas Konchenko, on a solo walk in space as he orbited the Earth, because he had disconnected himself from the international space station in what appeared to be a political act. A man in orbit. Living on borrowed time.

A few hours of air left, if that. Christmas Eve. At midnight –
or in just a few minutes, according to the calculations of his
oxygen supply – he would be dead.

Sarah and Henry.

BRANKA
HAD SWALLOWED
ALL
HER BOMBS.

Hadn't let a single one fall. We had gone to see *The Hurt Locker* at the movie theatre in Union Square, in June, and we had talked about the things you have to swallow without saying a word. Our armour is not all of equal thickness. The threat and the gunshots come most often from within. She believed that the things that remain unsaid and bottled up somaticize into cancer or some other serious illness. She had an uncompromising policy with respect to the truth, and like Jules Renard, a nasty compulsion to always want to say everything. And when things blow up, you just have to count the bodies and tend to the wounded. In particular, to stay with them. She would stay with her victims, as much as possible, to take care of them. Branka and her pharmacy dispensing love.

She never wanted to hurt anyone. She digested the grenades, the shells, the mines and the rockets that had been sent her way. If some move out of harm's way, dodge them or reflexively turn their backs and cover their eyes, she preferred the implosion. Sparing those close to her the shock wave.

She'd gotten pregnant the second time we'd seen each other, after the diner in Jersey City. The night when she'd had to go to throw up during the meal. I had found her touching. Sensitive. Yet she seemed calm.

I had assumed she was allergic to iodine because we'd eaten sea urchin. "No, it's what's going on right now that's doing it." I will never fully understand what she really meant to say. Perhaps she had just figured out what we were.

"Promise me that you'll never let me hang your stuff up to dry on a clothesline with my big flabby arms." I had answered that should we ever get to that point together, we might actually find it kind of lovely. It was one of the rare times where I'd been right to say what I was thinking: a man's love for a woman also means loving time and the traces that it leaves on our bodies and other places. Like the wind and the rain, it weathers us. In the best sense of the word. A patina.

I told her again that there is only one tragic drama in America: our emotions. The true victims of a great calamity are our feelings and perhaps those of the people closest to us. Nothing more. No group, no gender, no race, no kingdom. And certainly not ideas.

She smelled of saffron and sometimes mango. She smiled when we made love and kept her eyes open; she liked to look me in the eye and she managed to see beyond. It showed. Her eyes rolled when the pleasure became intense. She was beautiful like that. The impression of being understood in bed is worth more than all the gold in the world.

Other times she smelled like fresh tobacco. Just at the base of her neck. And I liked to stick my nose under her arm. I wasn't looking for the unpleasant odour that we try to hide, but the smell of desire or need, like when you're thirsty.

It seems that when you love someone, a mechanism in the brain diminishes the disagreeable and makes it desirable. Is it the same with beliefs? It seems that incense asphyxiates us and causes lung cancer. It also seems that when love is unconditional, we are willing kill to protect the other.

THE
GARAGE.
I WOKE UP
LYING

on a sofa bed in a place that smelled of dampness, cigarettes and diesel fuel. I'm like Harry Potter: I tend to faint whenever the situation gets too intense or meaningful. I was a bit ashamed. The TV voice was still telling the orbiting astronaut's story. My thoughts became clearer. Everything was true. It was the 24th, maybe the 25th already, Branka was dead, I had a son and I had gotten drunk. My phone was flashing. Blood on my hands. Visibility reduced. Jesus of Nazareth should have been on all the radios and televisions in the U.S. of A., not Stan.

A badly staged social collage: Sarah and Henry's interior decoration. An unintended retrospective. Or an ingenious scrapbook, perhaps. I've always liked flea markets because they restore my confidence in the existence of the Universe.

Old calendars were tacked to the walls. A crucifix; a yellowed photo of Ronald Reagan and a black-and-white of Jackie Kennedy; a working clock whose sound was reassuring; the scent of a fabric softener sheet, Downy or Bounce, that filtered through the other odours of dampness and fuel-oil; a '59 Corvette poster; a plastic Virgin Mary; a rosary; a baseball; a portrait of Pope John XXIII; a faded picture of Farah Fawcett, mechanically signed in black ink with a heart under the name; a framed photo of a young soldier in his combat uniform, proudly posing with his weapon. Dozens of lights, all turned off. Skeins of yarn and knitting needles.

A green cup with steam rising from it sat on a metal stand, above a candle. Plants everywhere, an empty yellow pack of American Spirit cigarettes. The smell of mould mixed with those of tea, tobacco, and the dusty heat of an old electric space heater.

I thought I was dreaming of happiness and avoidance when I saw Sarah Miller from the back, a long dress in some anonymous solid colour. I was reminded of a dream I often had as a teenager in which I was raping a young Hassidic woman. And it always started like that, in some indistinct place, like the back office of an antique shop or a kosher bakery in Brooklyn. I see her from the back, she is working standing up and bending over a counter, and I sneak up on her from behind. I grab her violently, hooking one arm around her neck and raising her skirt with the other. The force of the movement confirms the intention, making it crystal clear. She was beautiful, I think, with a scarf on her head. I am pressing my upper body into her back and I bend her over, pushing her face against a plywood table. Her thick glasses are all crooked, crushed against her flour-dusted face. The white collar of her shirt sticks out above the brown wool jacket. She is wearing flats. I tear her stockings. She says nothing. I pull at her panties and the seams give way. Perhaps there are some little moans from time to time, so faint in fact that I am not completely sure what I've heard. And maybe it wasn't even a rape, because she didn't scream or say anything at all. It seemed instead that she was crying, but then again, I never saw her tears because I ran away immediately after penetrating her, even before I'd ejaculated.

Sarah and Henry had lived there since 1980, since Ronald Reagan and his anti-strike law. That's why people love America's Republicans: common sense always prevails over communism. We saw it a few years later with Mikhail Gorbachev and the USSR.

A home in a dilapidated old garage with cars that were demolished, stripped or simply rotted away by time. Garbage all over. Actually, not really garbage, but hard-to-identify items collected from sidewalks. Containers of paint, tires, rims, broomsticks, tar kettles, plastic and glass bottles, an old washing machine, a boot, empty bags, full bags, wet cardboard and a thousand other bits of American debris that had been bought and discarded. And a sign: *No parking. 24 hr. active driveway.*

"Feeling better?" she asked.

"Yes," I said, but I was only being polite.

I was neither better nor worse. "What am I doing here?"

"My husband and I found you, sitting on the ground. You were talking to a fire hydrant, just across the way, in the snow. I think you had too much to drink." Pause. A siren in the distance. "Can I get you something?"

Why are people nice? Why are people nicer to strangers than to their family, their friends or their wife?

Henry Kane, Sarah's husband, was a Vietnam War veteran. He believed in and loved his country before becoming sick at heart. It's better that way because when it begins with rebellion and you end up loving and maintaining that inner hatred, you can quickly become a caricature. "True dissidence comes from an unexpected disappointment and a desire for reparation." Branka was reading Solzhenitsyn's *In the First Circle*.

46

This must also hold true when faith is a disappointment: its morals, love, political or economic or religious systems. It's hard to be invincible.

"Love cannot be divided." Branka again in May. "It can be multiplied, added to or subtracted from, in serious cases, but it should never be divided, dividing it is unfair, it weakens it... Love is the opposite of all powers."

She loved the music of the Yeah Yeah Yeahs, a group from Brooklyn. She often sang – or shouted, in the style of its vocalist, Karen O – lyrics she'd invented to fit their tunes: "I'll make you want me," with a French accent. "I hope I do, turn into you."

I am a generic man. No patent on me. I am worth nothing more to another person than the wealth that I can produce. My real value is in fulfilling a role without completely understanding it. Not exactly like an order or obligation, but more like an unwavering faith. The worst is not that we believe in falsehoods and in the thousands of charlatans who surround us with their theories about reincarnation, a great beyond or an all-powerful principle at another level; it's that we simply do not have access to the truth. Because think of it, Branka, there are still people out there today – and it's such nonsense – who believe that men are stronger than women. There are still religions that insist that the real power belongs to the word of *man*. You can't always catch up once you've fallen behind. The tortoise and the hare. Do you remember the fables of La Fontaine? We like to learn lessons when they serve our purposes and prefer to forget others because we think they're thwarting us. A huge amount of humility is required if we are to trust in progress. The illusion of moving forward. Like soldiers. Left, right, left. Left, right. Rest. We rely heavily on the orders we receive. Hitler must have been an intelligent man in private. But intelligence isn't connected to anything. The truth couldn't care less about common sense. And as long as justice remains unaware, it will continue to try to maintain its equilibrium with equal amounts of success and failure and it will have almost as many chances to be right as to be wrong. Its moral authority comes from another world, always projected into the future. And that is called History. The problem with Hitler was that we demonized him. Really shouldn't have. Therein lies the mistake. They should have shown us a man who was kind to his loved ones or his secretary. That way, we would have known that monsters and assholes can seem nice enough. That they too are capable of tenderness. That people like them and appreciate them in daily life. And then it gets easier to recognize them and try to kill them. Without making headlines and without warning. So that in the aftermath, life will go on without a hitch.

My century's morality is too flexible, like the whore in Amsterdam's red-light district who asked me, "Suck or fuck?" When I said "Fuck," she replied in accented English, "That's what I prefer." And two days later, when I answered the same question by saying "Suck," she again said, "That's what I prefer" in the same accent.

Hard to make sense of it all. You're dead, Branka.

The last time, I heard your voice, very low: "I'm going to come." Arched, facing away from me, hands against the wall as if you were pushing it with all your strength, your head down. I will hold on to the sight of the small of your back and the vertebra we call the nape of the neck as a memory of pleasure.

What do any of us know? How many of us would truly know how to make it all the way to the end?

"...One day the things close to us will appear far away. That's how you'll know that time has passed, not just for you, but just because it has, as it is wont to do, simply and in silence, for everyone, indiscriminately." So she'd said.

She had prepared me for all this. I am convinced that she knew she would die before me in New Jersey, on Christmas Eve.

I had always believed and known myself to be lacking hindsight, to be too absorbed by the day. No objectivity. As a result, I hated people who record their actions in time as if they were artifacts. Some authors do it. They quote themselves. They don't realize that people are laughing at them. We always come back to the mask game.

You know, Branka, the truth of the matter is that we're not quite as fabulous as they tried to make us believe when we were children.

Dear Cinderella, I often dreamed that I was forcing open your thighs; I dreamed about you, too. You resisted a little at first, but you quickly understood that I was stronger and you spread them. I always loved fairy tales.

Wonderments are for decorating churches, palaces and sometimes the clothing of kings and bishops who celebrate their power in the mirror. I am handsomer than you, look at me. We forget that vanity is born of a false sentiment. Pride may also come dressed in a robe. Even persuade us to line up on Friday and Saturday nights, Sunday afternoons or on rainy days, singing like the Jews, naked, encouraged by the Nazis to docilely sing as they went to take their showers in the gas chambers. We can also buy oversalted popcorn and sit down to eat it.

They took your body somewhere, to a morgue or a laboratory. They tried to understand but they will never really understand it all. And since everything we create originates with us, memory also fades. We can't do a back-up of our recollections or of sad and happy moments. A few rare and fortunate times, there is art. And still others, there is an homage to briefly bear witness. That is why it's so hard. You took with you the sound of bullets whizzing by, the redolence and light of war, and the cynical smile you had on your face when you listened to John Lennon naively singing about giving peace a chance. You didn't believe in it. You said, "Peace is man's oldest cash cow." And no one, certainly not I in any case, could contradict you because one never contradicts people who have lived through a war. Particularly if they're rich. They believe that they're invested in a duty of remembrance. They create works for the stage, write books and make films. We believe them to be immune from stupidity. You do not contradict the victims. And especially not the persecuted, and especially if their bodies bear marks of violence visible to a camera. We subsidize them. Truth that is only skin-deep.

You were good for me, Branka. You made me a little more human because you didn't need explanations or discussions.

From now on, I'm going to do it your way. Faced with a sushi menu, I'm going to put a Japanese smile on my face and order only the makis that have a connection with love: May Flower Love, Sweet Heart, Love Dancing eel, Crazy Beauty tuna roll, Perfect Baby love roll, American Dream roll, Hawaiian Marriage roll, Valentine roll, Wonderland Love roll, Rainbow Kiss, Spicy Little Mermaid roll...To tell the honest

truth, they're the best. Just don't look too closely at the ingre-
dients.

Sarah's voice still echoed in my ear: "You're sure you don't
want anything?"

THE
FIRST TIME
WE
MET.

Good Friday, April 2nd. Montreal. The engagement party.
She had looked at me in disbelief when I told her I worked
for a U.S.-based company called Antimatter. In French, Anti-
matière. Anti-subject, to translate it properly. The company
charges huge sums of money to erase all digital traces of a
subject, a news item or bit of information that is circulating
on the Internet. We have access to all the source servers. The
business is officially located just south of Baltimore, in an
industrial park built by the National Security Agency. NSA.
Supreme power with no accountability in an imploding
empire. We enter two, three, four, five words into the soft-
ware. Then we inject it like a vaccine into the source servers
and next thing you know, anything from near or far that
approaches the associated words disappears, everywhere,
until even first-order extinction is achieved. Antimatter
spreads like a virus. But instead of creating a new piece of
information, it eradicates anything related to it. It erases. By
replacing the kernel's internal connections with the thing
you want to eliminate. It's a new generation of vaccines.
Anonymous. Pure computer science. A humourless language.
Stripped of affect. The antithesis of words. Ferociously effective. Anonymous. Aggressive. Like a ghostly herd of Trojan
horses. The polar opposite of memory. Our main clients were
companies struggling with "negative" scientific studies. We
do not deny anything and we do not lie. All we do is disappear information. We are anonymous.

"Do you remember how Zhivago dies?" she regularly asked me.

"No, not really."

"After a monumental love story. The greatest of stories and one whose grandeur its society should have to acknowledge, in the streets, in the newspapers...?" She caught her breath: "Well, one day in the tramway, he's hot, he gets off at the next stop and collapses in the street. Face down in the midst of all these people who ignore him. He dies anonymous in the middle of the city." The greatest modern love story, overlooked and undervalued. "That's where the wound is: in the wretched embarrassment and humility of sentiments great and small that thus die of heart failure, lying face down in the dirt."

"OBVIOUSLY,
LIFE
IS
EASIER

in front of a television or behind a plate glass window, when you hear only the muted sounds of other people's chatter." Then she looked at me in silence. That was her response. I had just asked her how Sarajevo had seemed from the height of her apartment.

"The worst thing about the way we picture a war that keeps its distance from us is that it succeeds in making reality look like a fresco, like a work of art or a far-off scene. That's why we have to experience everything up close...or to be more accurate, that is why I detest men who use a telescopic sight to kill people. I *hate* snipers. I prefer close-quarter combat. With fists or a knife." She'd put her mouth on mine and then said that she missed the pink Chiclets gum she had chewed as a child. You can't find it anywhere anymore.

STANISLAS
KONCHENKO
DIED,
SUFFOCATED

to death by the cosmic void. Once he'd exhausted his supply of oxygen. A few billion of us had watched his fatal orbit on Christmas Eve, 2009. He died at the speed of 28,000 kilometres per hour, just over the Antarctic. An unquestionable Guinness record. All over the planet, amateur astronomers tried to see and follow him with their telescopes for a few seconds as he circled around the Earth. A satellite body visible from here below. Stan.

Nobody gave a damn about Chechnya. People talked only about this man in space who was going to die for a cause long forgotten. Proof once again that death eclipses the daily routine. We remember people who set themselves on fire or go on a hunger strike; we admire the act but quickly forget the reason for it. Oh, yeah! What was the reason, again? It was a spectacle. Unique. A first. Fuck the cause, but the *form*! The form was without precedent: the very first time ever that a man would die *not* on Earth. To forget that we're starving for meaning. We would base works and chronicles on it. A man suffocated from lack of air circles around a planet that appears blue precisely because of the oxygen in its atmosphere. His body will never decompose. He will be embalmed by the vacuum and the cold. An eternal ellipse. Millennia. He has joined the tons of orbital trash that evolution and our conquests have produced. Like ideologies, like the one whose uniform he wore – a Ukrainian flag on the right shoulder and a Chechen flag on the left – and that he seemed to be trying to defend. Except that, back on Earth, ideas moulder after a few decades, after one or two successes and a handful of failures. He was still in love with a woman who hadn't loved him for a long time. He would have liked to tell her in person, tell her first about the hate and then about the love. He had hoped to make amends. He had hoped for redemption and for all the words he had never managed to force from his mouth. Fragile and condemned. Horror and magnificence in the same body. The media's attention was much more concerned with the first outer-space suicide than in the apparent political statements of a terrorist. Stan had had two appliqués embroidered to represent his origins: a Ukrainian flag for his father and a Chechen one for his mother. But the cameras had immediately focused on Chechnya, thinking they had found a critical explanation. They were wrong.

I often asked myself if it is easier to die during a settling of accounts. He had all the time in the world to shed his load as he floated, counting down the seconds remaining. Our youth in Saint-François-de-Sales. The years he spent in the Russian army, medical school, those few months in Sarajevo. Her. The years in Paris. The dream of becoming an astronaut. Then her once again.

It kept my mind occupied and even reassured me to know that a dead man was circling over my head. From that day on, there would truly be something up above us.

Stan Konchenko was my best friend when we were boys.

BRANKA
ALWAYS SAID
THAT IF
ONE DAY SHE DIED

in some senseless way, it would be the Vatican's fault. She swore that she could prove that God does not exist and that she was only missing a few details to make her case.

"When I'm not pregnant anymore, I'll prove it to you." Her proof began with bread: "Poor people are the first proof that God doesn't exist."

I was willing to believe her. She had a weighty past on her side: the former Yugoslavia, a rape, a shattered life, a third language, ideas, feelings of love – particularly because of a few novels and poems. And she had an extraordinary lucidity, which very few people possess. Especially when she spoke.

The first thing I will forget is the colour of her eyes. Maybe blue, maybe brown. After only a few hours, I already don't know anymore. I saw through them. In the beginning, I didn't want to risk seeing myself in them. It took me two or three weeks. Perhaps it was a survival reflex. That was enough for me.

They say that people who make love on the summer and winter solstices have a better chance of surviving the end of the world than other people do. A strategy for modern witches. One of my faults is that I believe it. I like these old wives' tales. By default also. Like a computer technicality. *Par default/by default?* is the only true ideological advance since Kant and the duty to struggle against our nature. We are ants in the service of a queen. No changes expected because the system functions without requiring us to do better. Death.

We no longer believe by conviction but because we are logically obliged to do so. Automatism.

"And to whom will you prove God's non-existence?"

"You. That will be enough," she replied.

At the same time, in early autumn 2009, in Montreal, in a molecular biology lab at the Université de Montréal, a Haitian physicist demonstrated that it was mathematically impossible to eradicate biological life. Impossible. Period. All the destruction models that we've tried to invent are obsolete. This will continue regardless of what we may think and beyond all justifiable predictions.

Life was once explained by the virtues of chance, but now we must imagine quite the opposite: try as we might, using every possible means, to destroy all trace of life, it will remain a hypothesis. What if we created a god on the basis of this concept? Through its antithesis.

It is simply impossible that life does not exist.

Branka always told me when she was going to have an orgasm: "I'm going to come."

"Shhh," I would think, "If you tell me, I'm going to come too, before you." Have the courtesy not to tell me until the last second. Say something like, "I'm coming." No future. You have to watch your verb tenses. You shouldn't say, "I'm going to come," but rather, "I am coming." When you're waiting for something you really want, you miss it.

"There are millions of people who live on their archives. Immobile and dusty. Content with a few joys and a few sorrows. Hypnotized by hope."

"And after God, what will you do?" I had asked half a minute later.

"I'm going to go after happiness."

She had laid one hand on her abdomen and one on my head. Two maternal gestures, like the "quiet" sign we make, an index finger against the mouth.

"The problem with happiness is not that it doesn't exist. The real problem is how it's marketed. They show us its traces in the sand, saying that that is the path we have to take. We have to follow in its footsteps. Millions of books, millions of films, millions of minds like sponges that sink into the quicksand."

I will miss you, Branka.

"What defines us all, without exception, is a principle of belief...and that's what dies when we pass away. Just as the heart is an involuntary muscle, so the consciousness, by default, must also believe that it is involuntary and therefore guided from somewhere else." She had said this, still out of breath, one of the first times we'd made love, her right hand between her thighs to stem the flow. I had placed my hot, satiated hand on her perspiring chest. And I had felt her heart beating beneath her breast, just as she'd said "involuntary muscle." Her uterus must also have contracted. Another involuntary movement, no doubt.

AS WE
WENT DOWN
THE
STAIRS

of the apartment in New Jersey on December 24, 2009, she had said, "You know why, even in other lives, eternity cannot exist?" And then, "Because there would no longer be any morality between us: we could rape each other or kill each other or steal from each other without ever fearing reprisals." Her last words. One hand was holding the banister and the other was putting on lipstick.

IN
SAINT-FRANÇOIS-DE-SALES,
A SMALL VILLAGE
FIFTY MINUTES

south of Montreal, my friend Stanislas Konchenko was called Stan Kay. His parents had fled the USSR in the winter of 1969. His father, a weight-lifter, had won a silver medal in the 1968 Olympic Games in Mexico and then took advantage of a competition in Italy a few weeks later to "jump the Wall." He settled in Quebec because he'd seen images and a documentary on Expo 67. A farmer's son on the Soviet Olympic team, he – with his wife, a Catholic nurse born in Chechnya – had decided to rebuild his life in Canada, where the land stretched out as far as the eye can see, just as it did in his homeland. This new country, brimming with hope, was an immense forest with fertile plains. He would manage. He would do what a man had to do: start a family, as men had done before him, and feed it. As honestly as possible. Tired each evening, resting on Sunday.

Stan was born on April 9, 1970. Nine months to the day after Neil Armstrong had walked on the moon. That's not the kind of thing you can make up.

At night in bed, we'd talk by the light of a flashlight until his mother or mine came to tell us for the twentieth time that it was very late and that we should go to sleep. We were at that age where the hour has nothing to do with fatigue or sleep.

We built whole cities in the sand for our little cars, cities criss-crossed by roads, highways and tunnels. Several dozen Matchbox and Hot Wheels cars. That was the theme of our play: cars. Later, we'd gather up these toys until our hands were full and to put them away, we'd hurl them pell-mell into the black plastic Sealtest milk crate. Where they stayed until we invented another world, the following day.

We built thousands of cities under a giant Manitoba maple, whose limbs we climbed and in which we could balance for long hours, hoping that Stan's older sister would come home from school and decide to change her clothes in her room. Especially in summer, in the hope that she would put on a bathing suit. Through wear and tear and anticipation, our feet had rubbed the bark off the branches as we yearned for any stolen glimpse of flesh. A gift that became a magical memento, especially in bed at night, when fatigue does not always get the better of children.

We were in the same nursery school class, the only time we ever sat next to each other. It was a small village. Just one class for the first year of elementary school. The other years, when kids learn to read and write, the teachers separated us, as a precaution, they said. We used our scissors to carve cities and cars and airplanes and space shuttles into the varnished yellow wood of our desk tops. We were eleven years old when the space shuttle Columbia made its first flight in April 1981. Stan had been given a replica of it, a scale model to glue together, for his birthday. We assembled it on the kitchen table that same night, following the instructions to the letter.

We were always together. Playing marbles and dodgeball, in the park, during vacations. We played hockey, like all good Russian and Canadian boys. His life was also my life. We lived through the same times. Frogs, grass snakes. Jumping our BMXs and Green Machines, putting nickels on the railroad track, the giant drain pipes into which we always went a little farther, models to assemble, Lego blocks, sunburns,

Kraft Dinner with hot dogs, a copy of *Playboy*, yellowed and creased. The summer we were fourteen, in 1984, his parents managed to get him a visa and bought him a plane ticket to go visit his grandparents in the USSR. The other end of the world.

That was the first time my heart was broken. Stan was going to experience things somewhere else without me. Everything had suddenly become too big, adults severe and unjust. And this Russia that was, at the time, still Communist and "evil." We imagined it as grey and poor, with faces full of sad misery.

My parents had told me that the Russians lined up for a whole day to get toilet paper. Another whole day to get milk. And still another to get a dark-grey wool sweater. We made fun of Lada cars and a Belarusian farm tractor that a lowly neighbour had bought second-hand. Every time we saw it parked and at a standstill, we said that it must have broken down.

Stan returned at the end of the summer. But not completely, after all. He came back taken away from us. As in, my life here and the one over there. I know now that when you subtract all the lives you might have in a single life, the result is often a negative number. The connections we inherit are much stronger than the ones we build. Such ties are much easier to cut than to uproot.

Then one day like any other, three summers later, he told me he was going to continue his studies in the Soviet Army. We were seventeen. It was just before the Berlin Wall fell. The rules had been relaxed and the old countries welcomed their returning sons and daughters, no questions asked. I remember seeing heat lightning in the sky. Horizontal. We smoked a joint at the town rec centre, just next to the fire-house. He had repeated it: "in the army." Since elementary school, he had wanted to be a fireman. It was agreed. I was mad at him.

And then he left. The hardest thing to understand was the difference that appeared where there had once been only perfect accord. Stan was brilliant. He would certainly become a doctor or a high-ranking officer. He had a kind of intelli-gence that few others possessed. He almost always under-stood everything immediately.

The Eastern countries, at that time, were the West's third world. The official postcard for the absence of happiness: the meagre salary granted by the State, the total lack of culture, clothes all the same colour. That was how America pictured the other system. Serious, sombre stares. The Coal Age.

Part of me envied him. All boys dream of the army. Soldier. It was an identity. One that takes many years to develop. I felt both admiration and a stab of contempt for the business of war. And a jealous desire. The best soldiers are the ones who always live on the ground floor of morality. And Stan was not a soldier. He was too smart to personally carry out this primary function. To me, it seemed to go against his nature.

When all the conditions come together, and we do not know why, a man's true identity is always revealed to him. The milk left on the counter goes sour. Invariably. That's what truth is: curdled milk.

We continued to write to each other. On paper. I kept all the green envelopes. Stamps with images of Leonid Brezhnev and Lenin. He completed medical school in four years. Then he decided the army was boring and asked if he could leave. Far from the stipulated number of days. The Iron Curtain had been torn down. The West had forced its way in. Stan didn't want to become an officer in the military. He quit the official army. He wanted to get closer to the conflict. His mother was Chechen. We thought that he too was Christian Orthodox, and Stan never tried to refute the idea. His mother despised the Chechen rebels, who were all Muslims. He had wanted to go defend his mother's religious values right away. Somewhere else.

Christians. Against Christians.

He ended up in Yugoslavia with Serbian soldiers, believing that he cared about an ethnic and moral conflict in a country with no natural resources. He joined up with the Serbs. Much more of a militia than an army. With a paycheque. A mercenary's salary.

The two of us had spent hundreds of hours together, firing at targets with the pellet guns we'd gotten for our tenth birthdays. We were normal boys. From apples, 7UP cans, aluminium pie plates, giant cucumbers and pumpkins in autumn, all the way up to twenty-five-cent coins at fifty metres. From a distance, Stan was a better shot than I was. We pretended that he was neutralizing the enemy at that distance while it was my mission to run toward the target and finish him off. We'd set up an overripe pumpkin or melon as a head atop a scarecrow that we'd made from worn-out, outgrown winter clothes stuffed with hay. Stan always hit the body. He could assess the effect of the wind on the projectile and make the necessary adjustments. Ballistic intelligence.

Of the former Yugoslavia, he knew only what the media had reported. A racial conflict based on religion. A real one. No fair play. With a more or less central command. Those are the worst wars. Dirty. Metastases scattered just about everywhere. Even to remote villages. Orders from headquarters were watered down along the too-long chain of command or were ignored. Factions formed, the social contract became the memory of an ancient and rather vague idea, and the distance from the centre revealed the unchanging nature of man, his violence.

Because of a jealous desire for happiness. Stan had chosen his camp.

STAN
AND
BRANKA.

I am the bridge between the two. Branka will never know it. Stan, yes, and that is why he's dead. I didn't have the strength to tell the woman I loved that the guy up in space who was going to die on Christmas Eve was one of the soldiers who had raped them, her and her mother, in a suburb of Sarajevo at the end of August 1992. Nor the most odious part: that in Paris, she had fallen in love with this same man, the one who had impregnated her when she was scarcely more than a child.

"Don't resist too much, just enough," he'd told her mother when the two soldiers calmly entered their apartment. They put down their weapons and removed their caps. Branka had just turned twelve.

"WE
ARE CAPABLE
OF
HIDING THE TRUTH

from ourselves to make life easier," Stan had told me one day.
Sometimes it works, other times we accept this fact and
move on. The cat's out of the bag and we look the other away.

"And doubts?"

"What about them?" I had answered Branka.

"Are they a part of everyone's life?"

"Why do you ask?"

"Because I want to know if they disappear, if I have to be
suspicious of them, wait for them, chase them away or culti-
vate them."

"Where do they come from?" I remember having asked.

She had smiled and looked away, concluding, "It's like the
moons, you can depend on them." She liked doubt the way
some people like being afraid.

When she was six, she believed that each night a different moon passed in the sky above her, and she would speak
to it. One night she simply asked the moon how it was
doing. Another time she told the moon that she had learned
to write "zebra" in school that day. Zebra was a really complicated word. It was the last word of the alphabet in her
notebook.

And then one day she dared to ask her mother if the
moons would always come because she had more and more
things to tell them as she grew older. And her mother
answered that only one moon passed overhead, night after
night, according to a twenty-eight-day cycle.

She wasn't angry at her mother but at the order of things over which she had no power. She thought herself foolish to have confided all her secrets to the one and only moon.

I understood Branka a little, I think. We want to find a meaning. For ourselves and for others. To be moved and transported by something greater. There are times when life is just lived. It no longer tells a story. That is the deceitful quality of the representation: wanting to reproduce that which we already believed to be true. Another way of existing. Or an excuse. When all the rest obeys only the orders that we can anticipate, we know that the struggle was worth the effort. "Art is nothing but the watered-down imitation of time, formalized, aesthetic and not really necessary." And she had moved her mouth toward mine, saying, "Shut up and kiss me." Her lip gloss tasted of peppermint.

I remember her story about the Christmas carp and I think about all the people who know nothing. "We're as mute as a carp," she had once said.

"What? As a carp?" I'd asked. She was talking to me from the bathroom while she brushed her teeth. I hated when she did that.

"Every Christmas, one of my mother's brothers went to fish for a carp in a pond, fifteen minutes from Sarajevo. Three days before the 25th. The carp is a lazy fish, fatty and rich, and like the potato, it has saved millions of lives. So following tradition, the fish is always on the menu the night before Christmas."

But instead of killing it by hitting it on the head with piece of wood, she'd explained, her uncle would bring it back on ice and once home, he would slide it into the apartment's bathtub. Had to keep the fish alive until Christmas Eve.

"I remember the fish's slow, repeated yawning." And she had added, "When I took the subway as a little girl, when I passed by the churches and mosques, when I watched people line up or read newspapers, or desire an object, I'd think back to that poor carp who had, as he left his pond before being plunged into a enamelled cast-iron bathtub full of clear luke-warm water a few days before Christmas, the same illusion of being alive as he did in his muddy pond." The poor fish believed it had been saved from a death by asphyxiation in murky, brown water.

Branka and Stan were very similar in their lucidity. She through the calming distance created by the accumulation of days, he through the violent need and wish to make amends by getting close to the centre.

I am only the link between the two. Indispensable. The keystone of a Venetian arch.

AT
THE FIRST
APPOINTMENT
AT THE OBSTETRICS CLINIC

where her pregnancy was being monitored, Branka had told me that for her, the invention of God was an obvious necessity for survival, as uncomplicated as it was apparent. She had added, as if for herself, "Obviously we're going to believe in something greater than ourselves! For the first three years of our lives, we're entirely dependent on the person that brought us into the world. We're indebted to them, for everything from the smallest to the biggest things. When the primary requirements for survival become the involuntary responses of life, it's only natural that later, in adulthood, those reflexes from early childhood turn into beliefs and become ritualized: from a poop-filled diaper to hunger and tiredness or a sense of wonder, the mother becomes a source of satisfaction. Therein lies the first untruth. The origin of the wish fulfilled."

"And you'll notice that in every society, the people's degree of belief is inversely proportional to the advancement of women...the more men subjugate women, the more devout and pious is their society."

I believe that I loved her. I mean the kind of love that lays bare the flesh. The only demonstration of our self-discovery that is not egocentric. That state that makes you want to be with her. To want to hear her, whether she is quiet or shouting or whispering. That thirst for emotional intelligence. Not like a memory or the 292nd email you've exchanged, but in an accumulating present. The state that crystalizes us. It is here and nowhere else. Maybe it happens to everyone at one time or another. But then, no, maybe not; it happens only once or twice each century, and the rest is the business of a few individuals trying to portray it. Again and again. We change the names, the costumes and the characters and lean again on the supporting structure, which has itself remained the same since the very beginning. There are stories, like stone beams, that will last five or six centuries, and others that are made of cardboard. So few of them are structural.

I felt guilty that I had suddenly noticed the enormity of a love at the moment when it would cease to exist. I guess that's why people take photographs. The reminder of the event is that much more beautiful. As if it were in their cataloguing that events take their meaning. At the very moment when we are no longer in the same present. A hole in a woolen hat on December 24, 2009.

What if there had been more life among others than with me?

I would have liked to collect the trophies of war without having to kill. Without losing someone I love. The honours without the risk of danger. I convinced myself that there were billions of us who cruelly lacked determination. Everything is known in advance, like the trajectory of a planet that rotates on its axis, forever repeating itself. Yet there is a centre from which we grow increasingly distant. We will end up forgetting it by dint of having expanded space with new and ever-more-effective telescopes. The absolute and invisible epicentre is a gravitational force. We know when we're getting closer to it: doubts subside for a fraction of a second and there are no longer forty different ways to go. And for most of us, it often happens when there is an illness, a birth, a man's desire for a woman, a wrenching heartbreak, time that crumbles like cement, wrinkles in the skin or the death of a loved one. Or a kiss on a bench. The programming is sad. The other items of the emotional schedule are not terribly original. Repeats. As regular as comets.

And we always cry at the same place. And we always laugh at the same place too. And we always tell ourselves "I should have" at the same place.

Stan had wanted to tell her millions of times. But, like an asthmatic whose lungs no longer exhale, he suffocated himself.

Branka. You're dead. You have a son. Somewhere, someone will raise him as his own. Let's hope that the new parents can work things out for the best just as we would have. Because that's something else we don't talk about: the role of genes. It's still only rumour, but so many defective people reproduce along the way. Conversely, so many perfect people get broken along the way. You always told me, as you pointed to vending machines with an "out of order" sign taped to the glass, "It would be so much easier if we could attach such signs wherever they're needed."

FROM
THE TIME
WE
WERE FIVE,

Stan and I spent every day of our summer vacations playing together. At twelve, we had identical bicycles: two silver, five-speed Free Spirits. At dusk, we'd go to the sand pit, into the woods or to the houses under construction. Between the two-by-fours and the beams, in the framework structures. We felt good in these open places that had yet to be partitioned. The scent of spruce. We talked for hours. We used the pretext of action and games, but it was the thousands of hours of conversation that kept us together. That shaped us.

At the end of Rang Saint-Joseph was a pond a dozen metres wide, where as early as mid-July, the frogs were getting big enough for us to kill. Stan had come back from his vacation at Virginia Beach with some firecrackers. A true and precious treasure. Cherry bombs! Firecrackers were like naked girls: a gift you dared not hope for. Against all expectations, like a gold nugget or an old *Playboy* magazine, warped by years of humidity and found in an old abandoned barn.

The firecrackers came in packages of ten and we always calculated the best way to make use of them. No wastefulness. Some days we lit only one; on other, more extravagant days we lit up to three. We would catch frogs using a fishing line, a hook and square of red fabric for bait. Anything red: plastic, cardboard, a scrap of cloth, just so long as it was red. The frogs didn't bite, but they were curious and would get close enough to a bit of cloth for us to catch them, yanking the line to catch them on the hook. Then we'd tie the firecracker to the frog with some baling twine, saying, "*Ave,*

Caesar, your frog salutes you!" It made a sharp sound, the crack of a whip. Stan turned his back. He never went to see the casualties, whereas I found them to be half the attraction: I had to observe. We were normal boys in the face of death.

I no longer remember if we closed our eyes when the frog exploded. We probably did because I have no recollection of seeing it happen. Maybe we plugged our ears. A protective reflex. A brief second. Our brain is skilful. Clever, too. It usually manages to close itself off from anything that can damage it. That's what we hope for. Or at least that we're spared from as much harm as possible. Later, for adults, there's also alcohol. Denial may be a survival reflex. A hypocritical survival. When we don't want to believe in the atrocity of the moment, we first scream to ourselves words of disbelief: "Fuck, fuck, fuck!" An offence before taking the blow. Unless we're a complete and utter victim, with the cold barrel of a gun jammed down our throat, we should never rely on resilience to bury things that are imposed on us against our will. Hope survives. "The right to vengeance should replace the right to equality in the Declaration of the Rights of Man." Branka.

At night, when Stan and I talked for hours, we never mentioned the frogs we'd blown up.

AT
HENRY
AND
SARAH'S.

The sofa bed I was lying on must have been put into service on a thousand other nights. And on a few Christmas Eves. It had a thin mattress, with a depression in the middle so deep that I couldn't turn over or sleep on my side. I was pretty pissed off at the person, man or woman, who'd left his imprint there. Through a skylight improvised from a piece of fiberglass, I saw the moon behind a veil of clouds. It had stopped snowing. Only once had I seen the sun and the moon at the same time. It was in the middle of the Saint Lawrence River, on an island in the Île-aux-Grues archipelago. Naturally, I was moved by the phenomenon. When we can find signs that interrupt everyday life, we get emotional. A simple unexplained coincidence is usually enough to make us feel special. Other civilizations consider lunar and solar eclipses to be sacred. Divine compensations.

And whom will we trust too easily? In what respect? Will they one day manage to prove that the Earth is not round and that it actually is at the centre of the universe? Nothing up to this point has been able to prove otherwise. My planet is the smallest known point at the centre of the entire universe. Our equipment simply can't prove it yet. The failure of science.

Sarah collected dolls. I have always hated dolls. Stan and I hung his youngest sister's in the stairwell at their house, across from the front door, so she'd see them when she came home from school. They all met the same fate: Raggedy Ann, Cabbage Patch, Strawberry Shortcake and all her friends, even the ones with porcelain heads. We made slip knots, put them around their necks and gently pushed them into the void. It made a snapping noise. Sometimes the head and the body came apart, but their expression never changed. They had a factory smile or a hole to pretend they were drinking a baby bottle, and it gave them a louche look at night. Dolls, each and every one of them, are always far too happy.

Sarah was born in Kansas. But her family moved to Missouri when she was five. Raised in Saint Louis, she had kept nothing of Kansas but her parents' accent. In the early 1950s, French was taught as a second language in good American schools. She once met Cassius Clay. She had liked boxing ever since. She also liked to play cards, always with a magnifying glass that she waved before her eye, saying she was watching for cheaters. Even when she was playing solitaire. She must be funny. In the past, she never used to get out of a car before her man came to open the door for her. That was how it was. "A woman of principle," Henry told me. Gloves, glasses, hands on the knees and a handbag that always matched the shoes, colours and textures.

And then one day, something broke.

Henry was born in Montreal. To a French-Canadian mother and an American father. He used his American passport to enlist in the army when he was eighteen and shipped out to the other end of the world, to Vietnam, to defend Liberty and kill "Chinese" communists. He left happy and proud, if a bit nervous as he faced the unknown, since this was the first time he'd travelled. He did not return equal to what he'd been when he left. A shortage of humanity. And especially of faith. Not just the sort that inspires the pastor on Saturday, but the kind that can mark the border between a before and an after, when men are roused by the profound and ancestral nature of war.

In one sense, this fissure is what made him interesting for most folks. In other people's estimation, he had for years maintained the illusion of having existed because he'd gone to war. He had said, "Forget the jungle and the assault weapon; the biggest revolutions happened while I was sitting on a chair at home, silent, in love. Love rarely reveals itself, but leaves its traces, like bullet holes, and they bleed for a long, long time."

Henry and Sarah had written many letters to each other during the Vietnam War. Sarah's letters had been anchors for Henry and Henry's had been beacons for Sarah. The mailbox or the voice of the corporal who delivered the mail. Each time brought hope and anticipation of the invisible thread. Tied to each other.

Words had remained full of meaning and truth for the two of them. *It is broken promises that kill.* For years, Sarah had rewritten, in a little notebook whose pages she tore out, sentences that she had read here and there in newspapers, journals, magazines, essays, poems and novels. Like people who believe what they read. Then she glued these scraps of paper all over the place. On the metal cupboard above an old water trough once used to check tires for air leaks: *A peacock has too little in its head and far too much in its backside.* Or just above the garbage pail: *Ignorance won't kill you but it might make you sweat.* She had been a subscriber to *The New Yorker* almost her entire life, up until 1980.

I had gotten up to piss. I repeated the phrase as I left the bathroom, to memorize it, because I was still feeling the effects of the alcohol and Henry had looked at me as he raised his eyes to the ceiling. Through this gesture, you could see that he still loved Sarah. It's indifference that you should be wary of. My head slowly cleared. They were listening to both ABC and NPR. National Public Radio. They hated the religious stations. "Too busy with their debts and their fundraising."

And I began to have regrets. Or rather, to suddenly understand the numbers. It was through this subtraction that I felt I had truly loved Branka. That was yesterday. Today was Christmas Day, the 25th. I believe I had told her so often enough. Why is it only through its absence that we understand the weight of a presence?

Too Much Drama. That was the title of a book left lying on top of the toilet tank.

"AT
TWELVE,
I
UNDERSTOOD

that there was a ton of things we can never control," Branka had said last fall when I'd asked her if she would have wanted to change the past. "The past is just a former present."

I wonder if we can remake ourselves. I don't know. Can we reconstruct ourselves after atrocities? Maybe vis-à -vis yourself, you can; it's in the eyes of others that the tragedy remains one.

Henry had killed men that he did not know. Three. Three that he could remember. They had, however, been very far from him and had appeared tiny in his rifle's telescope. The same screen effect that the television has. Men less real than if he'd had to look them in the eye and feel their strength. In his case, the war never embellished life or its history. Was it more real in the time of bayonets? The death of others had only punctuated his own life. First by simplifying it during the first few months: a medal and the very clear impression of having won the final round.

Obviously, between the soldier who lives and the one who dies, there is only the concept of war. But beyond the political conflict and the power struggle, Henry believed that he was justified in surviving. For something else. For several years at least, he'd told himself. And now there have been many years since that time. With Sarah, without whom the meaninglessness would have been increased tenfold. Henry would have had a thousand reasons to exaggerate reality, to fill a void, but he chose lucidity instead.

Henry was a sniper. He could hit a dime five hundred metres away. At that distance, the man you're killing doesn't exactly die instantaneously. When he's shot, his chest is ripped to shreds, the flesh torn apart. The target becomes green, red and wet. The movement that animates the body evaporates within a few seconds. But the real death of a man, for the soldier-sniper Henry Joseph Kane, wouldn't come until several years later, far from that other world, when he would tell Sarah why he had woken up in a sweat every night since his return from the war. And then began the healing that would never end. He would never fully recover, preferring to put a finger into the hole that would never close up again either. Beyond his strength.

Branka: "The illusion of happiness is a trap that very few know how to escape. It's not made for everyone, we run after it for several decades, but it's like chasing a shadow. And if we think we've broken free of the trap, it's only because our leg has been cut off. We still believe the limb is ours, but it belongs to the trap. All this just postpones the expiration date. And the more you procrastinate, the more happiness you consume."

"You've already been a woman in another life," she had said one afternoon as she lay on the bed. I had asked if she believed in that. She never did answer. Words say the opposite of what they mean more often than silence does. Maybe that's a compliment. Or maybe she never said it and I just made it up.

Then she might have added, "You may already have noticed that even when they're ninety-two, or when they've accepted that they've become old women, they still put on lipstick, until the very end."

STAN
HAD SENT
ME
AN EMAIL

a week earlier, on December 19th, just before being launched into space. Even though we'd stopped seeing each other a long time ago, we still maintained contact. The days of our childhood were part of a distant past, but we always knew where the other one was. We wrote to each other from time to time. A message here or there. I had followed him from a distance, due more to courtesy than to pride. Out of respect, because we'd been friends when we were ten.

The email on the 19th was intended for Branka.

He asked me to tell her everything.

He explained his act. Not the one that the media wanted to believe in and therefore broadcast in a loop; not the one of a Chechen rebel who demanded sovereignty – he was Catholic. Nor was Stan on the side of the Muslim rebels. He was simply on his own side, that of a lucid man who sought to free himself from a past. To restore himself to the person he'd once been.

PARIS.
DECEMBER 1992.
SOFT MUSIC
FLOWED

from some unknown source. She couldn't see where it was coming from and she didn't care. A fairly comfortable lounge chair, the kind a dentist has, but covered with white paper that crackled with every move she made. A pleasant ambient warmth. The nurse gently stroked her arm and shoulder. Her legs were spread, her knees bent toward her, under a blue hospital sheet. The sedative made her sleepy. No pain, only the sound of suction. And the sensation of pressure coming from the inside. From an aspiration.

"We don't know how to abort a memory," she had said when she told me this, only her eyes getting misty. "Only distance, we hope, can do it, but then again..." And she had murmured words that I'm not entirely sure I had understood, but it was, I felt, something that you don't make a person repeat. Something like: "I still wonder if you should make a little girl pregnant with a rapist's baby have an abortion or if you should make a child carry to term the child of this violence."

Cases of conscience are always downstream from reality. Once the child arrives, it would be difficult not to love it. It's a biological force. And the fear of loving the consequence of an act of hate is an atrocity. We spend the rest of our time imagining what could have been, if such and such a thing had or had not happened. Like a reflex or a natural function, as involuntary as the heart muscle, the desire to understand, foresee or foretell that which otherwise might have been. When the idea of God's will simply isn't strong enough.

Before we love, we must destroy or kill precisely that which we might be capable or guilty of loving. Hence the modern and contemporary telescoping effect of technology. Physical distance. The truest form of separation. Branka would have dearly loved it if someone else had had the abortion instead of her.

It had always surprised her that since that year, she had invented a life, a future, a face for this non-existent child. Existence through the loss of it. She hadn't asked about the child's sex. She'd always thought it was a boy. Absences are also part of a balance sheet. Just as the negative numbers in an equation are found between parentheses.

She didn't remember the face of the soldier who would have been the father. She hadn't closed her eyes but she still wouldn't be able to recognize him. She had chosen to stare at the corner, the place where the two walls met the ceiling. She hadn't cried either. Not during. Strong as a dike. Only one crack in the wall. Yet it was through this tiny crevice that life had wormed its way in. A keyhole. It's true that everything is more terrifying when seen through a keyhole than when seen from an open doorway. She had long believed that the pressure that had begun to pull at her innards also had to exit the same way. Sometimes a perforation must be made.

Stan had recognized her. It happened in Paris in 2004, nine years after the war had officially ended. He knew instantly who she was. She who believed in fate the way people believe that happiness is in books or on a list of things you have to wish hard for. In a corner of her mind, under a thick layer of spider webs and dust, she had buried the face of the man who had raped her. Of the man she would henceforth love as only a twenty-four-year-old woman could love the future that was once promised to her.

Stan had gone to Paris to do a subspecialty in neurorobotics at the Salpêtrière Hospital. After going through that war, he surely wanted to heal others. He had gone back to the Russian army at Grozny after returning from Sarajevo. The military uniform and his adoptive language had opened doors for him all the way to France.

By 2006, fourteen years had passed since that small apartment in Yugoslavia that had housed a mother and her little girl. I had joined him in Paris for a visit. He had been practicing there for several years and had settled in well. He had believed himself to be mended. By himself. In his case, a course charted in advance would have been a blessing.

We'd gotten drunk like men who find themselves together again and are reluctant to talk to each other while still sober. We had found each other again. Because of the past. On the banks of the Seine in the 2nd arrondissement, he'd said, "I met a girl." He told me everything. It wasn't an anecdote but the beginning of a confession. Because men also fall in love. For different reasons.

He had fallen in love. The first time he'd seen her was at the grocery store; he'd been attracted by her head and neck. She had purchased a big apple that she had broken in two with her hands. She liked the acidity of not-quite-ripe apples. Maybe she wanted to look at the colour of the seeds to see if it was ready. Her face had hooked him, like one of those feelings of déjà vu that people think are signs of destiny. Wrongly so, because the future never mixes with the present. They avoid each other by default. Like the two ends of a seesaw: they will never be in the same place.

He had just watched her leave. She felt she was being watched and she found the guy appealing. So after taking a few steps, she turned back to take a look at him. That was all it took. A look. So few words. A certain restraint and a few gestures. As for the rest, what passes through our fingers, those are the anecdotes of the years spent as a couple.

He told me he'd been stricken by a thermal shock that rushed from his belly to his head. Like a billion needles. Attracted by her movements, her personal rhythm. By her solidity. All solid women are beautiful, I thought. Stan. Pierced by an invisible spear.

There are moments that don't get buried deep enough and from then on, you cannot think of anything else at all. That's when you realize that evolution is inconsistent because the mind doesn't always manage to control the actions for which we are responsible. Otherwise, it's just a girl with too much makeup on. During the evening, you want to marry her. Like a promise at midnight. The next day, you regret it.

Stan had told me, "That was the day I realized life had been good to me, but not to the point it protected me forever, at all costs." A dozen or so borrowed years, a reprieve.

The first time that you feel the crack. An open fracture.

Obviously, he had recognized her.

He thought about fleeing France. Europe. Becoming a sailor, a miner, a deep-sea diver, an explorer in the Antarctic, or keeper of the North Pole.

"Hello, Stan," he had heard behind him a few weeks later. She had asked him his name at the grocery shop. She had learned that he was a Canadian doctor practicing at the Salpêtrière. He knew who she was. It was better than every Christmas morning he'd ever had.

She had just said, "Branka," as she held out her hand. He had lowered his head.

"Her hand had so much meaning. Soft, firm, a bit cold, it was the hand of a woman, perfect. Thin fingers, perfect too, a gold band with a blue stone on the ring finger of her left hand, her hair tied back with a clear green plastic clip, a necklace of fake pearls twisted several times around her right wrist, a white hoodie printed with red hearts and a metal heart on the zipper's pull, her shoulders, her collar bones, an eggshell-coloured bra strap, no earrings." Stan had described her as well as any mirror could.

"You're going to be an astronaut?" she had asked because he hadn't responded. Because he was caught somewhere else, far from Paris and this Rue Vieille-du-Temple sidewalk at the beginning of the 21st century.

Under normal circumstances, Stan would have kept Branka a secret until his final confession. Seeing her again this way, recognizing her and fearing that she had also recognized him rendered impossible this life, which had still been almost normal a few weeks earlier. What if she was hiding her intentions? She could kill him as he slept, or worse, when he woke up.

As the image of the girl he'd raped fourteen years earlier began to fade, an updated version of the woman she had become made its appearance, the way characters are superimposed in the theatre. The little girl he'd raped now had two faces. And he had two lives, one of which had been entombed but remained impervious to decay.

Sometimes we have to accept what is. Give leeway to our instincts, in pain. Or under the anesthesia of obligations. A mandatory democracy. Imposed. Again by default. Because we're ready to assume the risk of a failure that already has no importance in the final reckoning. I want to love her. And perhaps even worse: I could love her.

The worst – because nothing like that happens as an isolated event – was the reciprocal love-at-first-sight. She had loved this man in one instant. And he, this woman. The natural upshot of this story, in this case, should have been a marriage, children, a few more smiles than tears, a possible confession, bodies that crease and bend under a heap of years and the death of one before the other or, in the best of scenarios, together in a plane crash.

As for love, the great love, we know right away. Its authenticity depends on nothing and no one. We are convinced. And that is exactly when Stan suddenly fled, after a vertiginous month with her, and become an astronaut for Russia.

How do you make love to the woman you've already forced? Men don't understand the internal fractures women suffer. Nothing. Zero. It is their wounds, the absences and the voids that end up defining them and provoking irreparable sorrow: a rape, the silences that run down their cheeks, an aspirated abdomen, love that crumbles like mortar or absconds, pulverized by an explosion. Toward the front, the back or even the sides, in a dimension that had been unimagined up until then. Relativity. Not even the euphoria of an invention. Simply put, a discovery. "As easy as love."

Stan never understood the nature of his own wound. He had refused all hope of reparation. He had chosen not to make repairs because he considered it a total loss. Too much damage done. The chassis was twisted and bent. Too costly to rebuild. We'll make mausoleum, as a tribute. A kamikaze. Under the silent guise of facts – a rape – he would take his own life. In a spectacular and masculine act. Obviously with the hope that Branka would comprehend the nature of his act and that she would forgive him. Because forgiveness, miraculously for some, is always imbedded, reinforced, in our foundations. Even posthumously.

I had received the message meant for Branka on the 19th. It began like this: "Branka, you remember a soldier..."

I never told her. I would not have been able to look her in the eye when she found out. My atomic bomb. Delete! I had printed it out but had put it in a trash bin just before I washed up on Sarah and Henry's doorstep. I had taken the trouble to make a copy and to seal it in an envelope. Everything contained in those nineteen lines.

Stan would never have asked her to love him again. Perhaps only to trust herself in the future. A police report, an accusation, a trial, a guilty party, an eternal silence, perhaps, an accepted hatred, a pardon? The idea of being rehabilitated had never even crossed his mind. At the heart of the confession, there is also resignation with respect to the future: no matter what will happen. "Come what may." There had been Stan, and now Stan-light-as-air. They would have had a child.

Branka had the gift of being able to stop what she was doing to say, "Look here for a second: I'm really with you" or "Hey, listen to me: I love you." She insisted that I look at her when she named things. It required such courage that this became the way I grew strong. And then in November she declared, "I have only been in love twice in my life: a guy in Paris, another Canadian, three years ago, and you." After a silence, because I had nothing to say, she added, "Thank you for that."

Me love you.

I
DON'T KNOW WHY
SOME
PEOPLE

and some lives are interconnected. For some mysterious reason, Stan and I had once been the best friends in the world. There are bonds that an unknown force creates for us, without our knowing it. An order beyond our comprehension. That is part of the invisible magic that can link us together. Period. Nothing more. Like being thanked because we love without intending to. Easily. A reconciliation.

Touched. Simply. Saying "thank you" for being loved. An act of grace impossible to define, but one that justifies all attempts to get close to it. Because it still has incredible power. Maybe that's all there is, between desires and forgiveness, to define us. The alloy in our chains.

I had added nothing to her "thank you," being content to hold on to the words that reverberated throughout my body. Guessing my discomfort, she launched a "Hey!" in my direction. I'd answered, "What?" and she'd smiled and said, "Nothing." She should have heard the echoes she was creating. For the pleasure of feeling the waves bouncing back and forth against my fragile walls.

We often love by dint of sentiments we cannot name. Especially men. For reasons that words cannot explain. At first, they're strangers like Stan and Branka. Brought together by violence or by the impossibility of describing other than through the sacred knots that slip from our grasp. An unknown language. Or frequencies.

"The most important thing about a lie? It's the horizon line. The scenery absolutely *must* inspire confidence." Like a hillside in Los Angeles.

Giving precise instructions, Stan had asked me not to reveal his identity until the 24th. I hadn't fully understood why until yesterday at noon, when every television, radio and world news report jubilantly related the condemned astronaut's story. His message for Branka ended this way: "Because too many people are satisfied with their past." The nineteenth line.

Branka never knew because she died just before he said his name.

DO EVENTS
OCCUR
NATURALLY

or are they instigated by us? Or by our beliefs? Is it possible that our wishes do come true? Would I have been in love with this woman if Stan hadn't raped her? Where and when does the meaning become acceptable for our limits?

Are we undeniably linked to others through every move we make, like that story of the butterfly that beat its wings halfway around the world from here? And more importantly, why do we have to explain ourselves with stories?

Every year, in August, I envied the life of my cousin who had a mental handicap. His parents owned a farm produce business and grew potatoes in Saint-François. From the time he was five years old, my cousin loved to "certify" the potatoes. He classified and downgraded the potatoes based on their shape and size. He worked up to twenty hours a day, first in the fields and then in the warehouse in the winter. He was useful. He handled those tons of potatoes with the same attention he would have had it been uranium. He had found a purpose. I envied his blissful – pious – foolishness.

He always gathered the first potatoes of the year on August 15th. On the Feast of the Assumption of the Virgin Mary. This year, Branka and I spent the evening of August 15th reading, in silence, on the same sofa. In love. I told her the story about my cousin.

I have always admired people who have faith. Blind admiration. Could be faith in anything: a sport, work, other humans

– there is a strength that radiates from those who believe. Like barometric pressure.

Branka had believed in Stan. She could not have suspected that he bore, heavily, a load that was going to destroy her. And yet he had been able to bear up under it, revealing nothing, for several years.

Stan had left Paris and gone to Russia a few months after having dated Branka. Because flight was the most logical solution. Nature teaches us that very early. A genetic reflex. For survival.

HENRY
DIDN'T KNOW
HOW
TO TELL SARAH

the things she wanted to hear. She loved him anyway.

Sarah had only to smile at Henry in the morning as he left for work to make him feel happy and alive. After the war, he had become a uniformed security guard for a big bank in Long Island City. Years of smiling and representing order while dressed in the stipulated clothing. He was the one who opened the doors to the public with his enormous copper key at ten o'clock each morning. He spent seven years of his life offering fake smiles and repeating banalities, pretending to be happy for a paycheck every two weeks and three weeks of vacation every summer. His efforts were entirely sincere.

Kilometres of humans day after day, patiently lining up, endorsed check in hand, ticket to survival, and thousands of comments about the weather outside, the weather tomorrow or the storm on its way. In the United States, people never talk about guns or abortion in public. Those are the last taboos.

Henry had never imagined that the state of war he had known a few years earlier, even with its atrocities, could be more alive that the tranquil, everyday state of peace in a free and tranquil country.

One day, in March 1969, he came home from the bank and spent the evening telling Sarah how sick of his life he was. She listened, getting up only to plug in the kettle and prepare a teabag. She spent half the night listening to the man she loved speak of his disappointments. It was more than a crisis of conscience: Henry wanted to withdraw from a conventional routine. Sarah followed him. Then she guided him. Neither one had worked since then. Essentially living off their society's surpluses. They had thought of one day writing a book about living happily on the margin, the margin that does not have to subscribe to the rules of consumption. And since the book would surely have been a success, they abandoned the idea. He knew that he'd make it to the end with her.

REALITY.
BRANKA IS DEAD,
I TURNED UP
HERE,

in an improvised house, a former garage at the back of a courtyard, standing in front of a bathroom mirror with rough square letters scratched into the glass: *Sarah + Henry, July 9th 1969*. That was the date of their union. Henry had remembered an old Irish tradition and had etched their love into the mirror's glass with the diamond in Sarah's ring, a ring that had cost him all his savings. He had engraved the date even before he'd officially asked her to marry him. One torrid, rainy night in July 1969, she had closed her eyes at Henry's request and followed him into a furniture store run by Chechen immigrants in the Green-point section of Brooklyn. When Henry showed her the mirror he'd just bought, her first reaction was to tell him it was scratched. He smiled. Then she read the date and their names, and she understood.

She put on the ring that he nervously offered her finger. They didn't kiss each other on the mouth. They held each other silently for a long while. They were bound together.

At the entrance to the furniture store, on a television screen, a Russian family was watching Neil Armstrong, the first human to walk on the moon, making his naive and ceremonious statement.

STAN DIED
AS PLANNED.
HE
SUFFOCATED

at one minute after midnight, New York time, on December 25th. The man on the radio pointed out that this was an extraordinary simultaneity: at the very moment of Christ's birth, a man died, strangled by the void. Maybe he was unaware that the fixed hour of Christ's birth has nothing to do with the time in Bethlehem, in Judea. "A sign," he said.

We take the measure of man by the chains that we invent. Stan had but one, strong and made of tempered steel.

His last intelligible sentence, spoken in French, was: "I am sorry, Branka Svetidrva." The media all over the world were now trying to find out who this woman was. Fortunately, she was dead.

I like to believe that he liked the way he died. In a happy aura of repentance, hoping to atone for a sin through its confession. How can a person achieve such an untenable lightness that he puts an end to his life? To cut a long story short?

He would have loved to be able to trust himself. A personal matter, like in elementary school when the Grade 2 teacher asked us to evaluate ourselves. Stan was always fair. He graded himself objectively, close to average. Five answers to choose from: excellent, very good, good, with difficulty and fail. I know now that, except for Mother Teresa, no one can do better than "with difficulty." If not "fail." We are overrated. By default.

One day, during the correction of a test, I cheated by erasing a mistake in Friday's dictation. Miss Annie had seen me and sent me to stand in the corner behind her so I could see the whole class. I remember a great sense of well-being because I had managed to remove myself from the otherwise intolerable routine of correction and because I had seen everyone who cheated while Madame Annie, her back turned, was writing the dictation's sentences on the blackboard. That was the first responsibility that I bore. The last was never telling Branka that my best friend was the guy who'd raped her. And that he had loved her as much as humanly possible.

On the morning of April 12, 2006, as she was completing her degree in art history at the Sorbonne, Branka went to turn in a paper on the nature of shadow in Caravaggio's paintings. When she returned to Rue du Bac, where they lived, she found the letter Stan had left on the espresso machine. A few words. He was going home because the army wanted him to become an astronaut. At the same time, he would continue to conduct his nuclear neurology research in Riga. Devastated, he was leaving her.

Branka hadn't cried right away. She had first wondered if they had truly been a couple because, she told herself, Stan should have talked to her about it. They had been living together for several months. This is what they say: couples make plans, have projects, talk about the future. A broken heart is often only questions left unanswered. They were happy even though she sometimes felt that Stan had absences. She often told him that he had his head in the clouds. "You should be an astronaut."

She had gotten herself a glass of water and then she had cried, alone. Not out of sadness or in the name of romance, but because she would miss his presence. She felt good with this man. It was that simple. Without turmoil and with so much respect that she hadn't immediately believed in it. Without knowing that the taste for the other is also a psychosis that gradually gets under the skin and stays there forever. Since she was twelve, she had wondered if she could endure the thought that one day, a man could touch her and love her. She had found the one through whom her healing could happen. She was going to find her centre again.

Branka had never spoken to Stan about the soldiers who had entered her apartment when she was still a child in Yugoslavia. One evening, she could have, she'd told me. It was after they'd been seeing each other for several weeks, in November. Just before their first night, naked together. They ate oysters at Marlow & Filles, in the 6th arrondissement. Stan told her that she was the most beautiful woman in the world. She received the compliment as a present, a gift. She was wearing a cadmium red dress imprinted with little white fleur-de-lys. No jewellery. She had taken off her earrings in preparation for this evening, thinking that it would make him focus more on her eyes. Stan would surely remember the fabric, the body underneath, dense and desired. Hot to the touch.

He looked into her eyes, letting nothing distract him. A dress that would be branded with love and desire. In the future, she would hesitate to wear it, too coloured as it was by these hours. Stained with ink.

When Stan had told her that she was the most beautiful woman in the world, she had believed in it as much as she believed in the wound that she always bore. It was the kind of evening when even the clumsiest waiters know not to intervene for fear of interrupting a man and a woman. She would have so liked to tell him of her pain, like an offering or a sacrifice. But she had remained silent, unable to start naming things from the beginning again. The first event, under a pile of others too heavy to move. Her eyes wet. Stan had probably thought that it was for him: eyes full of happiness. That is what she had understood and she had preferred it that way. With a smile, she had asked him if her mascara was running.

Stan had long wondered how he would manage to transform his guilt into desire. It was clear that only Branka could do this. He also believed, since that chance encounter at the grocer's, that you must always be careful what you wish for. Opportunities to make reparations often present themselves, but this one seemed like a miracle. He hadn't even tried to understand. He'd been given a second chance. The only truly important one of his entire life. Not his parents' second chance or the one bound up in the duty dictated by his paternal origins but rather, the one arising from an inherent flaw: human nature. His innate violence. A shameful reflex that we try to explain even before we try to eradicate it. The same way we plug up an oil spill in the high seas. Because every extra second adds to the disaster. The vagaries of an explanation.

Stan couldn't contain that which was slipping away from him. The fracture was deeper than he'd imagined.

HENRY
LOVED SARAH
THE SAME WAY
YOU LOVE A BOOK.

In the distant, happy perfection of having understood for a few seconds what they were. Together. It was enough for them to survive. And that was easier to do as a couple, they believed, because it meant sharing the duty to be alive. There are days when the same acts taken by a man and a woman are multiplied rather than added. On regular days, it's this: a glass of wine; you're beautiful; I'm alone, no, you're there, as alone as I am; are you coming to bed? We talk for an hour, we say nothing for a week, are we going on? On the other days, it is: the first glance, a prayer, a ring, a baptism, a vow, a miscarriage.

"Maybe these times will go on without us because they also exist without our knowledge. There are people who leave no trace of themselves other than debts and pollution." Authorized by religion. I agreed with her.

She often wondered which religious systems would best represent her faith, if she'd had one. "I have a weakness for Christian penitence. While some prefer the Islamists' rigidity and quakes, others succumb to a system of loyalty based on karma and bonus points. Christianity, even with the acceleration if its disappearance, is associated with a concept of guilt and an elevation of the individual because, for once, the burden of guilt lies with us. It creates accountability without placing blame outside ourselves."

Stan's reference points were blurred. He had fought certain men, directed by the beliefs of others, hoping to redeem himself, because he also believed that in another life he would have to pay for this one. No light is shed on the mystery. It is only beginning to reveal itself. And this is cause for concern.

ME.
I HAVE ALWAYS
LOVED WOMEN
WITH BEAUTY MARKS.

Perfect skins are theatrical. When she lay on her side, her bare back resembled a Lite-Brite game or an ancient map of the sky. I could connect these little dots with two dozen lines, it seemed, turning them into any number of animals, shapes or objects. One night, I had seen a spider, another night, a wineglass. One morning, I'd seen a handgun; one afternoon, a human form from the Lascaux Caves, like a Keith Haring graffiti man. "I love Keith Haring," she'd said the day before. I traced them with my finger. I don't know if she was asleep or awake. We didn't care one way or the other. We were content either way.

I don't know if we should invest in the future or the present. The future is overrun with reassuring uncertainties. Like promises that are never really meant to be kept. I never linked Branka to Stan. Nothing required me to do so. Even under threat, I would have held out because, for her, the idea of the future was an invisible thread that holds together the seat of your pants when you bend over and pull too hard at the seam.

There was no apparent nervousness the first time that Branka and I kissed. But I know that we were both rocked by hurricanes. That we were both trying to hold back. She had simply said, "I won't be able to resist this urge much longer." And then we had kissed.

I know desperate men who wished with all their might that their solitude be plundered. Without it ever happening.

There are days when I accept my own nature without protest and others when I have to put a knee to the ground to catch my breath. I remember her lips, the soft warm pressure of her mouth on mine, her cold nose, skin nearing skin, and the scent of this proximity, unknown until this moment. And I remember the desire.

When I add up all that I am, everything tells me that I'm normal. It seems normal to be here, in this exact place.

Is the love we all seek a drug we could wean ourselves off of?

I will miss you, Branka. We will have avoided plenty of pit-falls, especially those of daily life. The ones that suck the magic out of our enthusiasms. Even if the daily grind passes more quickly with a glass of wine as we give the kids a bath, help them do their homework or prepare supper, we are always in an antechamber. You already told me that you feel less alive waiting for a dentist appointment than reading an old Philip Roth novel. Lately, you'd been crazy about *Sabbath's Theater*.

"The courtesy of our daily actions is an affront to evolution," you said. Because humans control other humans. "We are no longer a contract but a social deficit." A fraud, perhaps.

We are also the multinationals that we point out as chi-meras. Behind the corporate screens, we look for men to condemn. Because the lynching of the similar, that's also what we are. "We." You insisted on the "we" because, in your opinion, immunity was the first sign of a shipwreck. The wreckage of profit, romance, temples and beliefs. "If we were nothing more than biological beings, we would be programmed only to ensure our own survival." But here we are, wanting things like happiness and delaying death as long as possible. Five millennia of dress rehearsals.

One of the first things that Branka told me during the evening we met was that her maternal grandmother, who'd had nineteen children, had only cried nine times during childbirth: when she'd given birth to girls. Because she did not want their lives to be like hers. "We shouldn't be talking about solidarity but about women's intelligence," I'd added, impressed by her story. You wouldn't have felt tears welling up in your eyes: you bore a son on Christmas Eve. Your destiny smiled upon you, you would have been right to trust in it.

Where do you go, if not inside yourself, when you've crossed over all the thresholds: a first kiss, an authentic night of love, a child, a promise, the death of one of the two? The Earth isn't really round. That was only the fashion of a certain era. Even if the astronauts tell us that it's true. You hold hands, you get used to each other. It's absence that we cannot adjust to. Even for the most atheistic of men, God once existed. Otherwise how can you explain His rejection? His absence is inconceivable to our level of understanding. His existence is easier to imagine than is His absence.

"Faith removes our responsibility," she had declared as she asked me to tie her shoes one morning in September.

THE
ALCOHOL
HAD ALMOST
DISSIPATED.

I remember sitting in the wet snow, last night, and seeing a man begging for money. He was scratching for pennies on Christmas Eve. In front of him was a poster on a bus shelter, announcing the New York Mega Millions lottery with its jackpot of $179 million. Some people see the exemplification of America in this disparity. They are mistaken. You would be disappointed, Branka.

Maybe there is no equality. Even less when we kneel before the dreams of others because our own do not exist.

THE FIRST
FEW WEEKS,
SHE LIT CANDLES
IN HER ROOM,

on the dresser whose poorly closed drawers overflowed with clothes. A bowl of pistachios still in their shells. There was the smell of burning wax and the perfume of flowers. There was a clock on the wall. Ten minutes before midnight. Our first encounters were all the same. We needed to be together so badly that we forgot to eat.

We had never talked about Stan in the beginning. Up until then, she was unaware of how the two of us were connected. She said that she had only been truly in love twice in her life. With him, that other guy, and then with me. Twice – that was already a lot.

"Maybe we've been fooled by hope. Eighty years, that's too little time to explain the rhythm that enlivens us. We like the idea of reincarnation because it promises a future and defines the past. But it purges the present of all significance, and besides, so many people have already been Catherine the Great or Joan of Arc." She wasn't smiling.

Had we been lovers in another life? Father and daughter? Had we loved each other? Hated? Had my son been my father at some other time? If so, then vengeance would have as many battlefields as it has lives to come.

"I hate the guy who invented the mirror," she'd said one morning when she got up. "Mirrors should only be used for cutting hair, putting on makeup or looking at yourself when you brush your teeth."

"But there are seven billion of us," she'd added as she opened her eyes with her thumb and index finger. "That's four billion more than there were at the beginning of the 20th century. We import them from where, these new souls?"

Are we a refuge? When the United Nations decreed that the six billionth human had been born in Sarajevo in 1999, she had wondered if there were antidepressants in paradise. We're not the ones who are cynical; it's all those who wish us the best with a one-way ticket. There's no wind and still we fly flags.

Branka always seemed surprised when I told her I loved her. A discreet questioning. Her eyebrows rose just a bit. As if she had to take the blow without losing her balance. Did she think it should be a one-way street, with no real need for reciprocity? Was it perhaps enough for her to love a man without requiring this same man to love her in return? Or the opposite? They were strange, these reasons she had for always remaining doubtful, even if she spoke with great confidence. Her norms. Or perhaps she had not yet met someone who comprehended the extent of her emptiness.

She used to eat orange peels. "All the vitamins are there."

She often discreetly touched her breasts with her right hand, as if checking on them. Wherever she happened to be. And when she wanted to tell me something, she always twisted a long lock of hair around a finger. One night: "You didn't notice that I've had purple hair since last night?" No. She just sighed as she looked at me. It wasn't serious; her silence wasn't an accusation. It might even have been acquiescence. One morning, I'd gotten up late and she was writing on her laptop, sitting in bed next to me. I had noticed that her fingernails were painted white. "I ran out of nail polish, so I used liquid paper, like I did when I was little."

The summer we were sixteen, Stan and I both liked the same girl. He knew it, I didn't. We'd just finished high school. Prom night. A rite of passage. The end of a phase. But especially a promise. Another one. In a pretty dress made of cheap bright-blue satin.

Her name was Loretta. One Saturday night in June, before the end of classes, a dozen friends had gathered in Stan's basement to watch a horror movie called *Evil Dead*. There was no warning. We were sitting on the floor, backs to the wall with our knees up. With a slow movement, she'd secretly and silently taken off one of her rings and put it into the palm of my left hand. Message received.

Later that evening, they left us alone in the basement. We were a couple. Even at sixteen, socially sanctified by the idea of life, the way a red-hot iron marks a herd. We kissed awkwardly. Now we were more than two because we symbolically bore the weight of our race and the only thing that it ultimately required: survival.

The day before, I'd been unaware that Stan had secretly desired Loretta since the previous year. Everyone had gone upstairs to the kitchen to eat pizza. When Loretta and I came up to join them, Stan was in the living room and he was drawing, his head oddly bent over the paper. Totally alone.

Now I understand his nervous trembling.

Withdrawal into yourself can also be an act of survival. A self-defense mechanism. Because it's first and always yourself that you must not trust. Stan was drawing in silence. It was according to that silent, autistic intensity that I could measure his violence. I didn't know what to call it at the time, but I knew enough to understand that Stan, without being angry at me personally, was feeding his demons. When we take its true measure, the distance between what we want to be and what we actually are is enormously disappointing.

That summer, Loretta and I were cut from the pack. Playing out at a distance what we had become. June, July, August. A whole life in ninety days, with a beginning, a middle and an end. Complete. Desire, love, drama. By September, we were no longer a couple. Separated by different schools and by differences as serious as our emotions. Stan and I got close again. We didn't talk much about Loretta, except for one night, a few weeks later, when I spilled my guts. Alcohol loosened the nearly adult hearts that housed our friendship. At one point, I said that I was sorry, that I hadn't known how he felt before that first night when I had seen him drawing. He asked me if I had loved Loretta, using the past tense, and he had clinked his bottle of beer against mine before I had a chance to answer. He must have assumed that I would say yes.

"Love is a perfect excuse," Branka had said, refusing to answer her cell phone as I lay with my head on her lap, pressed tightly against her pregnant belly. I was watching CNN while she buried her nose in Céline's *Journey to the End of the Night*. She never read French authors anymore so I asked her why this exception. "He's not really a Frenchman, he is a writer, first and foremost."

Stan and I loved the same women. The ties that bind us together define us as well. Even the transparent ones. For a fraction of a second. It's the explanation that we want to see.

Trusting people's natural goodness is not enough. One of Sarah's Post-its, glued to a crackled-glass bottle, which could also have served as a vase for flowers.

Branka went to pray in a ruined church before fleeing. The night before her departure, the soldier had broken her. She borrowed the Christian faith for a few minutes. "I gave him one last chance." The way you take a big breath before diving to the bottom of a pool to hurriedly collect as many pennies as possible. Wearing a blue dress, ballerina flats on her feet, kneeling amidst the worthless rubble, she requested a happy future for her mother and herself from a god that she suspected did not exist. She implored this god in her mother's name, in the same way that one might have acquired rights to the feelings of a former lover. Respect in an emergency situation. In a moment suspended in time. He owed her mother that. Pious and indestructible. On the first as on the one hundredth day of the siege of Sarajevo, no one could have predicted the duration of this dirty war between religions. Pivotal thoughts always prevail in those moments when the future backfires on us. Love in the atomic age. She was a pregnant child. She already sensed it.

During her escape to Paris, Branka almost believed. With each step forward that they managed to take and with each step that led them farther from Sarajevo, she felt the euphoric need to give thanks to something. While all these secondary stories are nothing more than accounts of an exile, she confused relief from the daily anxiety with a magnificence. Solaced, she gave thanks.

The love that we perceive is also a proof of existence. Even in discomfort or unease. There were days when I could have died at her feet. A chignon, a glance, a dress, a scarf. She could recite sentences from Malraux's *Man's Fate*, which she knew by heart, and smiled at the effect this had because I was clearly jealous. "Did you know it was the first book in the Folio collection?"

"No, I didn't know." And I had asked in a challenging tone if she also knew what the collection's second book was, thinking she would shrug her shoulders. She simply raised the Louis-Ferdinand Céline book she was holding, taking care to show me the title and to catch my eye for a split second. Then she went on reading. And I went on watching CNN.

I would have liked to know whether she had been as "intact" with Stan as she had been with me. Branka was an X-ray. I think she saw other people's fractures as well.

Do you remember, one now dead – this would help me hear you – that August evening at McCarren Park in Brooklyn when a firefly got into your left eye? We'd gone to see a Modest Mouse concert. That was the night I first felt your density.

You?

Since when?

The crack in a vow is visible. No matter how thin it is. It is due to this small opening that the world crumbles and is rebuilt. A nail in a palm.

"I will prove to you that God is an invention."

WHEN
THE ALCOHOL
DISSIPATES,
WE BEGIN TO FORGET

our promises again. Or we open another bottle to perpetuate the cult. I skimmed the surface of happiness that December 24, 2009. Branka's death was the most compelling approach to the nucleus around which I was orbiting. I was almost there. In the centre of the individual's humanity. In the centre of ours.

On the blank-screened TV, a man's solemn voice now recounted Stan's life, in chronological order, with a few rare family photos, I would imagine. Our childhood in the country – I'm sure there was a picture of one of our elementary school classes with Stan's face surrounded by a halo – then the army, medical school, Paris, the Russian space program, up to the military salute just before the rocket's lift-off. His Ukrainian father, his Chechen mother. Because that is how we must be defined: by a chronology. The codes and markers. Otherwise, if you mix up the names and dates a bit, we won't be able to make the connections for ourselves. Someone would soon figure out that the woman in New Jersey, killed by a stray bullet to the head and then gutted, was also the woman from whom the astronaut Stan Konchenko had begged forgiveness just before he died. What stroke of fate might reunite them? If not this so senseless one – the net we're all trying to weave to hold us together.

All traces erased and the sutures smoothed over. I was the only one who could explain the unlikely vanishing of two lovers who would also have had hate at the centre of their worlds. Each one's world like the other's. "As we witness the deaths of others, it is our own in particular that we imagine and then go over and over in our minds."

I remembered that I'd been born on the day Mark Rothko committed suicide, in 1970. The coincidence of dates, even in their flagrant inadequacy, manages to satisfy the mind. The thirst for origins is such that, even when we are dehydrated, there will forever and always be mirages.

It is also written that when Christ was thirsty, on the cross, a soldier drenched a sponge with vinegar and pressed it to Christ's lips.

I smiled thinking that Stan, who died at almost the same moment that the child was born, could be Branka's and my son. The thought of reincarnation can be a comfort. If Stan were our son, would he have come back to complete the reparations? To drink from the breasts of the woman who had once been raped in another life? And who now gives birth to us in this one? "Yet another fiction that strips away our autonomy. Maybe we choose to live in ignorance."

SARAH
WORE
A LAPEL PIN
THAT READ:

"We are safe, as long as the poor have faith." When she caught me reading it, she just said, "It was made in China."

Henry was preparing tea. His movements were slow and beautiful. The tea would be better because it would be made with care. He had managed to grow a tea plant under artificial light inside their shelter. They harvested and dried its leaves before steeping them in a bag made of mosquito netting. With devotion.

The tea was better because they believed it was. "Only in enamelled cast iron," Sarah had said, sounding both discouraged and appreciative. I had waited for it to cool and drank without ceremony, taking big gulps. I sobered up. They served me again although I hadn't asked for more. I would have liked being their son, at least for the time it takes to drink a tea. Honestly.

"We need other people." Written on my cup in a bubble over the head of Charlie Brown's friend Linus.

BRANKA
AND

I.

Our first introduction took place last April. "Pleased to meet you." Two kisses, one on each cheek. Then she'd said, "I don't know why I'm kissing you, we've only just met." Some Slavic or Eastern thing, I thought. And she had said, "Next time I'll find a good excuse." I hadn't said a word. She had smiled.

A birthday, Christmas, New Year's, a date. Maybe we kiss because we're nervous. Because of a need that we cannot name. To get close to another person. The force of affection. It is this thin film, benevolent and protective, that technology and kisses try to penetrate. A shield.

It just felt good to be with her. It was easy. No intention to lie. To her, I would tell the truth. She didn't tell me about her war that night but she told me about the anxiety she'd felt as a child. How much her mother had wanted to offer consolation for her childhood even before it all went wrong. She told me how she had hidden commonplace items in shoeboxes, a jewellery chest or behind the curtains covering the bookshelves: toys, marbles, newspapers, greeting cards, earrings, chewing gum, family photos, rocks she'd found. Her mother called her "my thieving magpie," with as much tenderness as concern.

I was touched by this young woman who told me about her childhood. By the humble narration of the life she had simply lived. Rare moments in today's world. No cynicism or irony. No moral, no echo. The simple life. Like the life, common and complete, of the poor when they do not complain about their poverty. And yet. I still knew nothing about Branka.

She wore a ring on the third finger of her left hand. A gold band set with a blue stone. "You're either Pisces or married," I'd said. "No," she'd answered with one word.

"Now I have a reason to kiss you," she'd said between the first cheek and the second, before leaving that evening.

"And what reason is that?"

"I had a nice evening and I'd like to see you again."

A man in love knows no hesitation. Even thrown off balance. Never. It's the only vertical certainty. "I'll be in New York next week," I'd said. And so we met in a diner in Jersey City. And she talked to me about *Doctor Zhivago*. And we took a taxi. And she got pregnant.

AUTUMN, 1969.
SARAH WAS
TWENTY-NINE
YEARS OLD.

She and Henry had gotten engaged with a ring in July. Eleven weeks pregnant. Her stomach slightly rounded just below her navel. Her breasts sensitive and hard. Eleven weeks of vomiting each morning. Exhausted from the moment she woke up. Smiling through it all because her nausea was worth more than the discomfort of having nothing in her belly. Something that dozens of months up until then had brought to mind, like a rosary of bad news since she'd known Henry and they'd been "trying." She had so wanted to have his child when he was in Vietnam. "Just in case," she'd said to herself. Henry would have survived through her had he died a soldier. And then through the child.

They had never really talked about it, death that is. They were not yet married but wanted to start a family. Especially Sarah. Engaged since the night a man walked on the moon. The same night she got pregnant.

Eleven weeks later. Henry was at the bank. He received a call. She never would have bothered him at work. That morning, she had peculiar cramps, different cramps. When he got to the apartment, Sarah was sitting in silence at the kitchen table. Daytime silence, rare and strange. She was drinking water from a beige ceramic mug. She had a big bath towel between her legs, her dress pulled high above her thighs. Henry said nothing. He exchanged Sarah's blood-soaked towel for a clean one. He kissed her neck and went to rinse the red towel in the bathtub. It was only on his knees, over this blood and this water, his head bent over the tap, that he cried.

For all the rest, he had to be strong.

He removed the mass of flesh, which had already stiffened, from the toilet bowl. He placed it in a shoebox lined with newspaper and laid it on the doorstep. He put on his grey felt coat, threw on a New York Mets cap and carried the box through the streets of the neighbourhood. He left it in a trash bin and returned home. He had remembered that, in the army, they had taught him that he must never physically "mark" the death of a comrade. Because the gravestone is either too far away, in another country, or too close, on a common roadway. Mourning can be experienced but once, and it must be perfect. Otherwise death becomes a slow cancer and we end up accepting it. Something we must never, ever do.

She had been prepared for millions of hypothetical calamities, maybe billions. But never for the two or three that count. It wasn't the baby, but the weight of her thwarted plans that crushed Sarah. She was pulverized on mute, as if hit by a nuclear bomb exploding in an archived film, destroyed by all the hope that a woman has for a child who would not exist. "The only antithesis of God," they had told each other.

What would follow would be hours, nothing more. Comforting Sarah. Making her feel, even when he was absent, that he was there. Comforting the woman he loved. Washing the towels. Cleaning the bathroom floor. Getting rid of the dress.

Neutralizing the actions and facts that could have become memories. Making all traces of a false start disappear. All this in the silence of a sorrowful understanding. Sarah and Henry wouldn't even allow themselves the luxury of assigning a meaning to it. It would be a long time before they spoke of it, not until today. Sarah had given names.. To everything. To all those details of which he believed he was the sole guardian. Sarah had experienced them all. She remembered, in a burst of empathy, no doubt, for what I had told her about Branka. Not necessary to confide her own sadness to confront the other. But some stories teach us how to live. La Fontaine, Romain Gary, Anne Hébert. Henry was impressed. Her silence. A time during which the weight became a gentle cloud. She had seen everything, his actions and his restraint. His efforts to save her from the thunderbolt, the sadness, the nameless blow, so that she would not have to relive even a single second of the penetrating sorrow. That is why she had loved this man. Seeing through him, this Henry who believed himself as waterproof as a lead shower pan. She had pierced him like a shock wave. "That is why I love you," they told each other. "That is why I love him," she said to herself.

Sarah knew. Henry admired her. There always comes a moment, long after the wearing and tearing of days and words, when being two means transcending each other. It is only at this point that the project of being a couple ends up becoming profitable. Before that, it's just an illusion.

Henry, who quite justifiably believed he had secretly experienced episodes of profound solitude, now found that he was being observed. His actions validated by the eyes of a woman with whom he wanted to step off the cliff. Sarah noticed the actions that Henry took in order to hide others from her. Since the beginning. Literally. As simply as possible. The gesture that needs no explanation. A reassuring omnipresence. A mother's kind-hearted concern during a night of fever. "Like what we imagine a god to be," I thought.

The indissoluble obligation to be a pair so that one of the two entities is all-powerful.

Sarah had looked at me, without smiling, without questioning. Just listening. An acquiescence with no subtext. "There are moments that have no need of us, eh?" Branka?

Henry stood up. He served me more tea. Lukewarm. Sarah asked me if I wanted her to reheat it over the flame. I said no. The actions that turn the pages. Others that mark the chapters and allow us to breathe. And others finally, like tourniquets that contain and numb the wound in the time it takes for help to arrive. It's when the knot is undone that the pain or the poison spreads, a moment when we have to be ready to feel the stiffening of the billions of needles that suddenly rise up in our veins. In the best of cases. As for the others, we'll have to pull their weight and tolerate the threat.

Henry told me, "It's easier when there are two of you." He kissed her neck as he had that day. Tenderness.

SUMMER 1986.
"FUCK!
SLOW DOWN, STAN!

Or I'm getting out..." I think I had yelled. It was unambiguous, in any case. We were sixteen. Stan had gotten his driver's permit first, in April. His father always needed him to go shopping or to drive the tractors and farm machinery on public roads. He had bought him a 1983 Plymouth Reliant K. This crappy car had no power and Stan always stomped on the accelerator to remind himself of that.

Where the village streets met, there was a level crossing with such a big vertical drop that each time we passed through, at the same reduced speed, our hearts jumped in our chests. Like when we jumped off the cliff behind my house into the Saint-François River in the summer. A reaction of biological vertigo. I remember that my father always asked us, my mother and me, if we wanted to "do the bump." Throughout my childhood, I said yes. Putting that blind confidence in my father.

Thirty metres away, National Highway 205 intersected with Saint-François' main road. My father never drove fast enough to miss the required stop. The pleasure of making our hearts "jump" always ended in laughter, "do it agains" and a stop at the corner.

Stan had raised the volume on the radio. It was the summer of Bon Jovi's "Livin' on a Prayer." He'd glued the gas pedal to the floor while pulling hard on the steering wheel. Then he had stared at the road straight ahead. Speed. "Slow down, Stan! Or I'm getting out."

When we jumped the railroad crossing, my heart reacted as it would on the best rides in the big amusement parks, with all the pleasure that safe, well-controlled fear can allow. Only half-fear.

The Plymouth's four tires left the pavement after the tracks. We were suspended horizontally for a second or two, giving the impression of cinematic time, when adrenalin distorts awareness and slows down the scenery flying by.

But when the car touched the asphalt, I really got scared: Stan still had the pedal to the floor, his hands welded to the steering wheel and his eyes focused even further away. It wasn't the train track he wanted us to do but the intersection just after it, burning through the stop sign, looking neither right nor left to see if there were any cars coming.

First, I stared at the ARR T/STOP sign, trying to make it magically disappear. Unsuccessful at 140-k. Ahead and to the right, an old barn; to the left, dense woods. The national highway with three numbers had no stop sign. A straight path.

Coincidences do not happen. But accidents do. I remember, the second before, looking at the intersection in the passenger's side-view mirror. When you're sixteen, you're blinded by the illusion that you're lucky to still be alive after something like that.

I wanted to get out of the car when I felt the car gain momentum. But secretly, I still admired Stan. "Risk is sexy," Branka had whispered the first time I told her she was beautiful, the time we ate sea urchins.

We didn't die that night, at the place where the roads intersected. I understood later that we rely too heavily on unknown trajectories and that, each time the battle takes place, the euphoria of victory justifies all the ends. Even when we lose, the shock wave becomes meaningful for the survivors. It's what we did with James Dean and Jackson Pollock.

It wasn't Stan I was afraid of. It was me.

LAST OCTOBER.
BRANKA WAS CLEANING.
WE WERE AT HER PLACE,

the Jersey City apartment that she shared with her mother. Her mother spent half the year in Sarajevo, from September to March. "It's her favourite time of year." Childhood memories were tied more tightly to it. Also because of the 1984 Olympic Games. "For once, world history was being made at home." It was in their backyard. Branka was almost four years old. Her father was already gone by then. He had only known her for eleven months when he was killed by a brick wall that collapsed on him at work. Save for a few yellowed Polaroids from the 1970s, she had no picture of him in her head. The first rendering she had of a man was that of an almost-naked body, dressed in a white loincloth, hands and feet bound and nailed to a wooden cross, just above her bedroom door. The same dusty crucifix that she had implored with her eyes when the soldier had forcefully dragged her into her little girl's room in 1992.

"I hope it's a boy," she'd said as she wrung out a rag in the sink. A pink elastic held her hair behind her head in a high ponytail, a bobby pin above each ear. I hadn't answered her.

I think that she believed in some other thing. Certainly in an other. But definitely not in the touristy clichés of the great religions. "If one day Saint Peter calls my name and if I'm not sure it's really him, I'll ask him to say my name again, this time with his head down and his feet in the sky."

"I detest baking cakes," she'd said right after that. "Because the sugar requires too much precision." She had just put a Betty Crocker vanilla cake into the oven. I approached her from behind. "Don't you come walking by my cake!"

The successful preparation of choux pastry or cinnamon brioches requires precise instruments like a scale and a thermometer. Nothing left to chance. "I prefer the science of uncertainty."

"Love is like a play," I'd thought. But it should always end in the first act. After a single performance. Now. We all have to strive toward a centre. "In fact, it is in this unique and perfectly circular gravity that one should die," she had once had me read from an American novel. Surrounding oneself.

Branka died within the realm of happiness. She will forever be deprived of several heartaches and a number of years. A telescope's lens would not have been able to enlarge her to her fullest extent.

TODAY.
MY GUESS
IS THAT STAN
WAS CALMER

than he had expected to be when he took his place in the rocket last week in Kazakhstan. A trip into outer space will never be a routine exercise, but he must have assumed he'd be nervous. And yet he would commit this act without a weapon or equipment of any kind. Hence nothing to conceal. The person carrying a handgun always has an advantage because it can easily be hidden in a coat pocket, but it can also be detected. Unless it can be made to completely disappear. Incinerated, encased in cement or thrown to the bottom of a river. Once it has disappeared, nothing is left to prove the crime. It no longer exists.

Even if Stan had been naked, no one could have seen the intention or the plan he had. The triggers of guns that kill men are first pulled in the mind, in concepts that are also the product of our evolution. So we assume.

He most certainly believed that I would have read his message to Branka by now. That I would have told her everything, trying to convince her or reassure her during his final fall. He most certainly would have found comfort in that. A slow and silent bomb, which he had carried almost entirely on his own since that Sarajevo suburb in 1992. As a heavy, shapeless force crushed him into his seat, he surely would have thought that the powerful thrust of the reactors tearing him away from the Earth's gravity was acting as a bloodletting and that the weightlessness of space would relieve him of another weight. His own. Not one measured in kilograms, but in guilt.

He might have looked back upon our childhood and imagined the moral obligation that I was going to fulfill. He told himself I owed him that.

I did not give Branka the words that Stan had written.

Stories from childhood always rise to the surface when we feel a calamity approaching. Maybe he thought about that Labrador puppy that we'd rescued from a storm sewer and saved from a slow death, or about the cat that he had tortured with his house key. Between our heroic acts and those that were cruel, we had been children who learned what life was all about.

We were eleven. With one hand, Stan had grabbed the cat's neck and the more the animal struggled to bite and scratch, the tighter Stan's grasp became as he poked the cat's sides with the key. A vengeance that he provoked and perpetuated. In a stupor, the cat finally stopped moving. Stan put it down and ran off. I don't remember now if the poor beast was still breathing.

I do, however, remember the slow, wet noise of the skull that cracked under my foot.

The rocket continued its ascent. Stan was going to cure himself of whatever was causing his pain. Anesthetized by the lie, the Novocain or the alcohol. It seems so easy just to lie to yourself to go on. "No, no, this won't hurt and everything will be better afterward."

The majority of us will avoid the one true instinct and the two or three feelings that count by seeking refuge in a physical consolation.

The tribal approach gets it right. Stan fought for a cause that was not his own. But it became his just the same. He did not choose it. He joined the Serbs, naturally believing in Orthodoxy. In humanity's darkest hour, which returns as faithfully as a planet. The dark hour that gives the order to kill everyone in the enemy camp. Women, children, the old and infirm. Sarajevo lost 10,000 citizens to the snipers' sights. Immobile, weak and civilian targets. As soon as Stan understood the issues and the utter senselessness, within as well as outside himself, he left. After thirty-nine weeks.

"Democracy seems to be the opposite of a system that has yet to be named." We were discussing communism. Branka had certainly been in the crosshairs more than once. This man, these men hadn't pulled the trigger for reasons all their own. A lack of courage? Out of envy, or deviance or lucidity? Are we really just moments guided by instinct?

Stan didn't shoot Branka in the garden in June 1992. He raped her at the end of August. That was enough. Later in October, after Branka had fled to Paris, he took aim at her pumpkins in the vegetable patch and blew all three to bits.

HALLOWEEN
DAY.

We were walking around Jersey City. She liked to walk with her round belly. Apparently it's good for the mother and the growing baby. Something to do with circulation and gravity. Even if it's easier to give birth standing up, babies come out of mothers stretched out on their backs.

Across the street, a school, a playground, a ringing bell, children leaving the building and parents waiting. A man dressed up as a cowboy and surrounded by people is selling dozens of pink, blue and yellow cotton candy cones dangling from some kind of wooden umbrella. Cars are double-parked, empty school buses stand idle.

"Do you think about him sometimes?" she had asked. "Who he'll look like, what he'll grow up to be?"

"No," I'd answered her. I wasn't there yet. She was smiling, looking off into the distance, wearing my Yankees baseball cap. As always, she had her hand on her stomach. "I would love to go to Turin this spring."

That's another reason why I loved her. Because even though she was an atheist, she admired churches; because even though she was an atheist, she wanted to see the holy shroud. "Things that manage to survive us in silence across the centuries define us more than our words and their intentions, even if it's to a degree that we don't immediately understand. We have to put our faith in something that endures throughout the ages." Branka had built herself of stone and mortar. And quicklime.

I told myself that I should leave Henry and Sarah's and go to Turin, to do what she had hoped to do.

THE FIRST
SATURDAY
IN
NOVEMBER.

"Time is the only thing that can explain us." She was reading David Foster Wallace. She never read anything but American authors. Cormac McCarthy, Susan Sontag, Joyce Carol Oates. Since Paris, she'd stopped reading French writers. "There's no one modern in France, they all write and speak in a closed circuit, defined by their borders and the memory of what they once were. They're one-way streets. Their definition of the present is built solely on a historical past. With its wine, its cheese, its skirt steak and its escargots, France is nothing but a giant museum with fabulous food." She had lived in France long enough, even hurt as she was by the man who had left her, to understand that "when a country's language gussies itself up in order to please, when it's corroded by the words of another, in this case by the American language, it accelerates its downfall." We sense the death of ideas through a language. We don't officially declare it dead. Instead, it dons a dress, adds makeup and wears high heels; it gets watered down and eaten away like a riverbank. It then survives through artifice, contest prizes, and the illusion that it's the queen of the ball. Life is measured in the kitchen, not in the palace. Branka and I thought that language was also gauged in daily life: do you need help with your bath? Or: did you see how that girl looked at my Hermès bag?

Branka believed that the Eiffel Tower would outlive the French language and French culture. The erosion of iron does not speed up, but it has its own pace. Immutable and constant. A millimetre every eleven years. The structure is unstable and a risk to public safety, the President of the Republic would say with sadness – with a heavy heart – and should be destroyed at the turn of the 22nd century. So it goes with symbols and marvels. And our bodies. We will rebuild another monument.

She never went back to Sarajevo either.

Your tears don't scare me, Branka Svetidrva. They worry me, but I'm not afraid of them. In early November, we ate in a restaurant in Brooklyn – in Williamsburg – called THE END. She wore a green maternity dress. "Like the Stella McCartney dresses this fall." Short, over patterned blue cotton-knit tights. I saw the skin of her thighs through the lacy netting. Full breasts. Cut just low enough to have an impact. A black bra, which I could also see. She ran a hand over her right breast: "Never break your vows."

And she took a sip of red wine from my glass. "They're the only things that count." She added, "Dance with me, here, now." I went to her side and took her in my arms, in silence. We didn't dance but we stayed there, holding each other, for several minutes. Her belly big between us.

"You love too much," I thought. I was wrong. It's not possible. Real feelings are never cynical. We hear it everywhere. In the worst case, they suffocate or are uncomfortable, but not here. Not here and not now. We exist a little more at this precise instant. Nowhere else.

I promised myself.

In your arms on that very night. I knew what you were asking.

We had arrived at this point. Not anywhere else. Gettysburg, Waterloo, Normandy, Pearl Harbor, Berlin, Stalingrad, Ho Chi Minh, Sarajevo, Pretoria, Kigali: we pass through the

131

fire. At this very moment. Prolong it. It happens only in love and in the intoxication of believing yourself eternal. Euphoria again. An American dream.

Two hours later she was folding clothes for the baby.

"Have you thought of a name?"

"No," I answered. "Have you?"

"I've always liked Emmanuel. When I started at the university in Paris, I read Kant in a philosophy class and thought that I could love a man named Immanuel."

And she told me that, in its most absolute freedom, of its own free will, the one true purpose of humanity should be to destroy its Nature. The only evolution possible.

I promised her that I would not break my vows.

I had gone to pee. I had spit bluish-red into the toilet bowl as I urinated. The wine. The same colour as her stockings. I had flushed. I spent my entire life thinking that at certain moments I would exist more than I had before or would afterwards. "Destroy our own Nature." Like Oedipus. Like Medea. Free ourselves from the chain. And from the soldering. Do not aspire to happiness, do not submit to its beliefs, prove the inexistence of God by tracing the outline of the empty hole yourself. This was now. I was at the centre. My centre. I had lived thirty-nine years. I would surely live at least eighty-three. Branka had lived twenty-nine years. She would only live twenty-nine.

She would have liked to go to Turin this spring. The holy shroud. I never understood why. I had her hat, with the hole in it, stained with her still-sticky blood, in my left coat pocket. "Someone commenting on John Paul II's next-to-last encyclical, *Fides et Ratio*, once said something to the effect that 'A little science alienates us from Him, a great deal brings us back.'" And then she'd added, "And too much reality forces us to remove ourselves from the rest."

"I just want to be understood." That's what she had said one of the first times we'd met again.

I also told Sarah and Henry that the private organization I worked for, Antimatter, could make all electronic traces of an event vanish by erasing the written reports of it found in the press and on the Internet. By focusing on the frailty of our memory and the little interest we have in others, this enterprise has achieved an almost perfect success rate. Stories of corruption, political scandals, accusations both founded and unfounded...my success is based upon the exact opposite of propaganda: the less we talk about it, the more it ceases to exist. We erase the sources, in blogs, press agencies, articles, even in online encyclopaedias. Information is linked to the truth as much as it is to falsehood. Indiscriminately. The equation no longer exists when one of the variables is removed. All that survives are memories, with all the weakness of their absent proof. All we have to do is make the weapon and the motive disappear. And most importantly, we remain anonymous.

The truth thus becomes a rumour, an urban legend, whose veracity we begin to doubt. There would only be, sometimes, certain loves or vengeances that could survive the absence and the passing of years that tempers everything. Especially vengeance.

"If we don't tell our stories, we disappear." Even if we do it for our own sake. Naturally. It's a mechanism for self-destruction. For birth.

STAN
WAS LIKE
A BROTHER.

The one whose life you live through. The one after whom you cannot imagine your days otherwise. This is also a form of love. After the vertical love of the mother, there are all those horizontal ones through which we are filtered.

In Paris, Stan had asked me: "Where are they, all those magic moments they promised us?" Because even in his second chance with Branka, he wouldn't find them. "They lie to us because we want them to." We can believe in something better and beyond this world. In destiny. In the world's magical instinct. In an order that is beyond us. A fairy tale. We lower our eyes. And we slake our thirst in the escapism entertainment provides. In its reassuring imitations of life.

Even with his idea of being happy with Branka in Paris, Stan had a war raging inside. Not a poetic, metaphorical war, but a hate-filled battlefield right in his very core. A mass, lodged in his gut. He'd thought he could get rid of it by drowning it in daily life. It didn't dissolve. It came and went as it pleased, between the whisper and the cry. Like a cancer.

We all have a dam and Stan's burst. He was nothing but a spectator, forced to watch, unable to look elsewhere, although he'd tried. Booze. The work, the studying. The others. But the price of forgetfulness was too high. He would be an astronaut.

He had believed that forgetting would allow him to live with a modicum of comfort. He had stopped explaining his misdeed years ago. Unable to figure out why he had done what he'd done. He no longer looked back. He understood all the efforts made to avoid having to justify himself. What a bacterial soup life is. Three or four random events, a few words and one conscience later. Rules and transgressions. Religions tell their own stories, invent their own beginnings and ends. Believing in them. The immensity of the void should be filled by a metaphor for the self. We're going to have to live through another century of social solitude.

Stan could have had faith and become a devotee the way other people become junkies. Or he could have drowned himself in work. Or gotten lost along the way. Become a bit of human wreckage or a Nobel laureate. Momentarily reassured by others. He decided, alone one night when he could not sleep, that he would face his responsibility with the heroism of a righteous retribution: confessing to the world his culpability and his love. In a single sentence.

Ulysses refused Calypso's offer of eternal life. He preferred finality with his wife, Penelope, and his son. Simpler that way because the expiration date forces us to speak and to tell. To set our sights on the centre.

Branka: "Why do we have to comfort ourselves with small joys?" I would have liked to answer you: "Because big ones no longer seem within our reach. They're so simple and so rare that we fail to notice them." She added, "The spitefulness of great things artificially connects us to tiny spontaneous impressions of being happy. When a hand on the hip, a steady gaze, or a caress that comes out of nowhere are enough, in their grandeur, to prove to us beyond all doubt the impossibility of anything greater than ourselves. Cosmic humility." Belief or lack thereof. Branka swore to me that she would show me the empty chair of God.

Perhaps she'd show it to our son, but not to me.

And then this lightning bolt last night. In the explanation of this so-called "sudden" death, there would be as many gospels as blank pages. My meaning. My truth, right there, hidden like a pearl. And made up like a whore.

THE
LAST
HOUR.

Twenty-four hours later, I realized that staying with Henry and Sarah would only mean waiting for a touching aftermath that would never materialize. It was time to leave. I wouldn't have minded delaying my departure because telling our stories connects us to others. Them to me and me to them. And because saying the words is liberating. Not holding on to our bombs. Not holding on to our bombs. And yet it is the ticking of the detonator that forces us to be what we truly are. Do I cut the blue wire or the red?

Close to the final act. Far from Hollywood's felting intentions. Far from redemption and special effects. Away from this simplistic polarization that attempts to explain that which we are not. We are not in a duel; we are in a labyrinth of possible deaths.

"Like the gulf between the rich and the poor, the difference isn't any deeper today than it was at the dawn of time. It's just that it is overflowing with those we've thrown into it." We were walking along Fifth Avenue.

Stan believed that the countdown on the launch pad would sever him from an evil deed. He had walked down one last corridor. Of his own accord. He thought about Branka. He saw her again as a child of twelve. He had often tried to push the scene as far away as possible. To bury it under billions of tons of cement. Radioactive. Now he had to replay it all the way up to the emptiness of space. He had also seen her again, as an adult, with him. In their apartment, at the bakery, at the museum, at night, in a restaurant, when she was slicing

137

tomatoes. He saw himself silently admiring her and wanting to love her to the point of forgiveness. Without her knowing. If only, without his asking her, by the most unlikely of miracles, she had just said, "It's okay, we're going on together."

She would never know. Dead a few hours too soon.

"We all revolve around a centre." And when we near the expiration date, of a planet or of a truth, forces send us off course. A perfect trajectory is an aberration. There are always deviations. It is quite possible that the only thing the mind ever invented is a straight line. Impossible, non-existent.

I doubt that Branka could have been happier or more healed than she was yesterday at the end of the day, just before she died. Neither one of us had any family in the New York area. We had decided to go for a long walk on that Christmas Eve. She had just said, "Taking a walk will be good for me." We had just made love. One last time. She wanted to walk. All I wanted was to keep her from learning the name of that astronaut in the sky high above us. Every TV in the world had been talking about him for hours. Live broadcasts. People would soon know his identity and would inevitably start wondering who *was* this Branka Svetidrva whose name he had spoken as he emptied his lungs.

Stan's death was luminous. The cold, empty space had finally entered into him. Into his values. In two acts. A magical rhyming. Perfect. As if harmony could be an atonement.

THREE
MONTHS
AFTER
HER MISCARRIAGE,

Sarah had decided she wanted to adopt a child. She couldn't summon the strength to start over from the inside or to endure another death. Especially not that. She had asked Henry what he thought. "Good idea," he'd said, without much conviction. He wanted nothing but the best for Sarah. If easing her pain, maybe even finding some kind of happiness, meant a child to love and raise, he would be there. As a father. Once the surprise and the strangeness of the idea wore off, he had told himself that this was what had to be done. They would raise the child to be a good person. Parents' promise.

Sarah had called the local adoption centre. A nurse had told her to come to the hospital for a meeting the following Tuesday. That was in February 1970. When she and Henry arrived on the fourth floor of Saint Mary's Hospital, they found themselves in the maternity ward. Henry didn't understand right away. Sarah did.

They signed three forms. The first concerned their marital status and their address. The second was the legally binding Adoption Form for the State of New York, and the third, typed out, required them to ensure to the best of their ability the child's care and education.

February 1970. Sarah and Henry left Saint Mary's. Henry with a brown paper bag of diapers, a bottle of formula and a blue-and-white flannel blanket.

Sarah was carrying a six-day-old baby boy in her arms.

She would have liked to ask the nurse where the child's mother was. Dead? Teen pregnancy? Rape? But she hadn't the strength to hear the response. Too many embers in her happy head. She had left the place, more deeply in love with Henry, herself and one other.

Not smiling, but with a responsible, silent joy.

Their son would have been the same age as me.

"The advantage of the parable is that everyone thinks they've learned something from it." That's what Branka had said one day when I'd commented that the Bible was an extraordinary work. You can also open it up to any page at any time and relate the ancient words to our present times. "I adore the Psalms, but I also love vampire stories, and Dorothy Parker's poems, with the same level of respect, and that's worth as much as Nostradamus."

She often had contractions. She would hold herself under her belly, immobile, then lie down until they passed. She stared at the ceiling.

"I'm still waiting for the definitive Opus, the one that will provide me with an explanation." She had searched in books.

JUST
BEFORE
LEAVING.

Sarah put on an orange fake-fur coat to go feed the pigeons. Night was falling. It had been almost twenty-four hours. How far to take the confessions? She and Henry had listened to my story with all the reverence due the secrecy of the confessional. With slowed movements, Henry struck matches and lit candles. The alcohol had worn off and was no longer any help. Without anesthesia, like in grandmothers' stories. Operating cold. The good old days.

The sound-only television was still telling the story of Stan's life, searching for an explanation. I'm not sure if I should have told Sarah and Henry about our friendship. Tell them that we had loved the same woman. Yes, *that* Branka, and the love that had linked her to Stan and would henceforth be known to the world. On the news, they also reported that a woman who matched her description had been found dead at the same time, last night, in New Jersey.

I restrained myself. We always expect the same reactions in the face of misfortune: crying, tears, a divine lack of understanding, a profound discontent that drives us to confess and illuminates the moment. These are emotional reflexes.

I will miss her neck. Her smells and the billion things that define us and bind us together for six or seven decades. Whenever she crossed her legs, she lowered her gaze. Before she got pregnant, she always slept on her stomach. She used bicarbonate of soda to clean the bathtub and when she ran out, she used toothpaste. Her alarm clock and her watch were always set fifteen minutes fast. She fiddled with the pendant on her chain whenever she spoke about the past or stared into my eyes.

You never had anything to prove to me, Branka. You'd won me over. In perfect admiration. I would have liked to adjust the line of fire. Make the bullet that struck you go off course. Or better yet, like a fairy-tale hero, take the bullet for you. A serpent biting its own tail. And I wouldn't die right away so I'd have time to tell you how much can be understood when you want it to be. I wouldn't have been able to explain you. My last words would have been relics of the past. Sadly stifled until the last note of the final music is heard. Lies, red-white-and-blue. Like at victory parades. Because half of the misfortune begins with us. It will be my turn to prove to you that God exists. In our story as well as in the purpose of a film's final credits. Still sitting on a red velvet throne, stunned by what we have just achieved together.

Explanations, even scientific ones, bring us back to the concept of a god. Whereas in the absence of oxygen, we can't even imagine understanding anything at all.

BRANKA
LIKED MUSSELS.
SHE SMOKED
FOR YEARS.

She rolled her own cigarettes. At one time, she'd even wanted to be a nun. Like all the women I used to know. To be married to Him, if only for a few moments. To find out if He exists. Perhaps marriage allows us to see if the other person really exists. Especially the day after the wedding.

One day one of her great-aunts, a nun on her mother's side of the family, told her that God had appeared to her on her sixteenth birthday. Since then, Branka had wished it would happen to her. An apparition. An irrevocable moment. The kind we silently hope could actually be possible. Lourdes. Fá tima. Medjugorje. Just that simple. "I think Kant forgot to tell us that our propensity to believe is as natural as being lazy or selfish," she had said as we were taking a walk one day last summer. The obsession of faith, like an old blanket that smells of the closet. The reassuring odour of mothballs.

We had never held hands or put our arms around each other's waist. Because we move forward more quickly when we're not holding the other person back.

"It's the disjunction that hurts the most." Between the promises we feast on to deaden the days. Like the ducks and geese that we force-feed to enlarge their livers. Between our prayers and the ones that are fulfilled, there is an entire universe. "Never break your vows." An echo. I will not forget. I swore that you would not suffer anymore. Neither through your body nor through the awareness of what you used to be.

I wonder if she knew. I imagine she did.

ON
JUNE 1, 1992,
SERBIAN SNIPERS
WERE SHOOTING

at anything that moved in Dobrinja, where the 1984 Olympics had been held. Stan was posted on the roof of a twelve-storey building. He was missing all his targets. Intentionally. He had held, in his crosshairs, dozens of civilians, regardless of their religion. A few old men. Women and children who were putting empty cooking pots and plastic bowls out on the grass and the sidewalks to collect rainwater. He fired next to them. "The worst isn't thinking that you might be a sniper's target, it's surviving a tragedy that's near at hand, like the death of a parent or a friend. The randomness of death was intolerable."

On December 25, 1992, Branka, sixteen weeks pregnant, was twelve years old. In Sarajevo, a ceasefire had been declared so that Christians could go to midnight mass. In the darkness of a besieged city, with no electricity or running water, people still went to celebrate in church.

On December 25, 1992, Branka had an abortion in Paris.

She'd menstruated for the first time in March. Just before the war. Just before the rape at the end of the summer. The Parisian relative who'd taken them in had tried to convince Branka and her mother to keep and carry the baby to term. This act of God. As violent as it had been. Because His paths are guided by intentions that are beyond us. But they adhere to a plan, it seems. One that escapes us at the present time but whose inevitability will one day catch up with us. She had said all this as she gently lay her hand on Branka's forearm.

The magic is in the future. In the reprieve.

Branka felt the child inside her. Certainly she felt nature calling on her to love him. She would fight it. Hormones and biology. She had understood the difference, aptly termed "the intention." But nature has no moral principles. Nature wants only to survive, as much as any fungus or rat. And all its means are justified.

Even if she allowed strangers to adopt the baby, which she had considered, she could not survive. Because she was also at war, against Him. She would fight, surrounded by soft music and under a fluorescent bulb's cold light in a Parisian abortion clinic. The nurse who had gently laid her hand on her forearm to comfort her could not guess that, behind the fixed, steely stare, Branka was focusing on a corner at the exact point where the ceiling met the walls. She had emptied herself out like a bomb that hits the ground.

Her tears flowed into her ears.

I
NEVER
TOLD
STAN

that I was in love with Branka. I told him only that, through the most providential of chances, we had met in Montreal last March, at a party given by mutual friends. We had simply been attracted to each other. I had immediately figured out who she was when she held out her hand and said her name. A deluge. How was this possible?

Stan had not answered my email. I waited several days for his response. Maybe he had silently wondered how it could be possible.

Branka was already pregnant when I told her that I knew Stan. At first I hadn't said anything. And then later, it was too powerful.

"He and I were good friends in another life," I had said in November.

"Have you heard anything from him?"

"No, I only know that he's a doctor in the army and an astronaut for the Russian space agency."

After a few seconds of silence, I added, "I can try to contact him if you want."

"No, to each his own life," she had replied. And she had gone back to her book, *The Road*, sitting in the corner of a blue sofa with her knees tucked under her. I never was able to say for sure whether she was trembling or if she was indifferent.

"There are days that we let slip away."

SARAH
AND HENRY
RAISED
THEIR SON

with all the love one could ever imagine. He died in Iraq in 2003, at the age of twenty-three. The final report from the United States of America's army chief of staff concluded that it was an accident. Friendly fire. An absurd death. A stray bullet, fired because the target had been incorrectly identified. "It's already difficult enough to look death in the face, especially if you have to look back at it every seven seconds."

Sarah had cried like a mother. Henry, torn between military loyalty and the whirl of his pain, told himself that none of this tragedy would have happened had they not adopted that child back in 1970. As if all the days of our lives were interconnected. They are not. It takes years to accept. Their dead son was merely a consequence.

Sarah told me that this child had become her own. From his first smiles to the baby teeth he lost, from the first day of nursery school to his first goal in a hockey game, from his entry into the army to the heartaches caused by other women, she had so wanted this boy and nothing could have predicted the love she felt for him before they'd met. We often become what we wish to be. A mother, a son. And we also often become what we dread. Someone who grieves.

"It will be seven years soon," Sarah said as I put on my coat, just before I walked out the door.

SUMMER 1979.
WE WERE
NINE YEARS OLD.

On our developmental path, this was one year after the end of the toy cars. Stan and I had clothes-pinned baseball cards to our bicycle tires. It made a noise like a motor because the cards vibrated against the spokes when we rode. The faster we pedalled, the more it sounded like a revving engine. We had collected sawed-off pieces of old boards and built ourselves a jump. The sensation of taking flight, of lifting off the asphalt, was intoxicating. And we raised our wooden springboard with big rocks and bricks that we found beside the ditch. Taking turns, we launched ourselves at full speed, chin lowered, pedalling with all our might to land even farther than before. I remember that Stan had said, "We should do like Evel Knievel." That meant putting someone's life in danger, extending the distance past all reason, making a performance out of it. In every relationship between friends, there are roles to be played. As in everything, never equal. I had said, "Okay, I'll lie down and you jump." I had carefully marked the distance of my last jump and told Stan he had to jump past it because that's where I was going to lie down. We always hear that the salvation of the species comes through the limits that we push. The fraud that is the Olympics, an illness in remission, a stopwatch, pain, a hamburger-eating contest, a bereavement, a jump, a belief or a Guinness world record.

Branka liked ice cream. One night, she had been sitting in front of her computer and had read aloud with a spoon in her mouth, "Death is the opposite of a centrifuge: it is the only thing that pulls us toward the centre. The gravitational force of grief. That of others, but especially the one we fear. Because it exists even without us: the clockwise movement of the minute and second hand. The crumbs that fall and horizontal happiness are only pleasant memories."

I know that Stan and I went further as a twosome. We would have stopped before the end if we'd been strangers to each other. We, too, were a couple. Friends. It helps us verify things. And it's in the eyes and actions of the other that we allow ourselves to discover who we are. Not in the trials or the failures but in the success that we hypothesize. The importance of the hypothesis. Crucial.

I watched Stan pedal with all his strength, with a strength even he did not know he had. I had stretched myself out far beyond the most distant mark. A calculated risk. Like the bet you make with the Heavens when you say "cross my heart and hope to die." I was wearing a white T-shirt with blue, three-quarter-length sleeves and Myrtle Beach written across the chest. Toughskins jeans and blue-and-white Adidas. I was more than a metre from our last recorded distance. When Stan's front wheel hit the ramp, time stood still. I saw him, his eyes focused far ahead, his hands welded to the handlebars of his blue chrome-plated bike. His feet had stopped pedalling when he left the ground. Suspended in mid-air, perhaps for a second. I also felt his back tire pass a hair's breadth from my forehead. Why does our perception of time change at such important moments? Why is there another rhythm? It's chemical, apparently. He grazed my side and landed on my right arm. I didn't say anything because he had crashed when he hit the ground, raising a cloud of dust, gravel, noise, crashing, banging and pain. He smiled anyway because nothing about this drama really mattered. The goal had been achieved: jumping past the mark. His two elbows and an ankle were bleeding. The scabs on his skin would bear witness to the exploit for weeks to come. The grey face. The hair stiff with dust. The pants torn at the left knee. We had conquered something and we knew it.

EARLY DECEMBER.
"DO YOU THINK
WE COULD
HAVE BEEN FRIENDS?"

She had just sat down.

"No," I said.

She had looked at me and smiled. And declared that the last man on Earth should perish in New York. In the United States of America. In the place that had once been a land of dreams and faith while waiting for something better to come along. In the diluted memories and nostalgic values of a political falsehood and shattered ideals. Violated. Another discrepancy. Faith, like the reflex when we're tapped below the knee. Like nerves that die several minutes after the heart and the brain. A spasm of prayer. Or like our hair and nails, which continue to grow several weeks after we're laid to rest. America's failure.

"I live in a city where a homeless man can walk down the street, opening all the empty pizza boxes he sees in the garbage in the hope of finding some scraps because he's hungry, while at that very moment another man, in a stadium that sells pizza, is getting paid twenty million dollars a year to throw and catch a ball." America's success. "I'm not being indifferent or cynical, it's the objectivity of my observation that worries me."

"I would have liked to live in a world where our values would have been respected, because there are more people who know Julia Roberts than people who know Mother Teresa, and that makes me uncomfortable." How do we extricate ourselves? If we are only as strong as the weakest link, we're dead. "And we're dead anyway. You know what?" she'd said. "The project is a disappointment. Not in the narcissistic effort of daily life, but in the hope of a new millennium." The vital signs are vanishing. Branka was pregnant. Are hormones also connected to ideas?

I LEFT
WITH SARAH,
WHO WAS GOING
TO FEED HER PIGEONS.

They had returned for the night to the little cubbyholes of an old wooden beanbag game, which had been converted to a dovecot.

"It's already too late," I mused out loud. "We're going to have to keep on consuming and increasing our consumption because otherwise everything will fall apart. We're wrong to live on the margins of capitalism and dreams; a slowing down of the economy makes more people poor and forces us to acknowledge the system's inadequacy. Whereas its acceleration makes more people rich, with the hope that one day the indecency of it nauseates them and causes them to vomit up a little of their extravagance on others. Then there would be poor people around to thank them." Sarah had nodded her head.

"One day, Perdiccas asked Alexander the Great when he thought that he should receive the gods' honours, and the king replied, 'When they themselves are happy.'" This was part of the promotional text on a cheap DVD Branka had just found in Chinatown. She had laughed when she read it. "Listen to this." She had gone on, putting the film on the pile: "The Greeks invented and contented themselves with several gods. As did the Romans. And the civilizations that followed also failed. They all failed. All that's left are their stories. As always, the need to explain themselves. In the disillusionment."

We loved to look at the displays of multi-coloured fish. "The most effective of contemporary stories, however cynical and critical, will seem obsolete to people in the future. We make fun of ancient gods and other people's gods. Especially immigrant gods. Just enough to kill. The mystery swallows us up like a fog. Let's just be satisfied with the fear of being lost. Or of being alone."

Branka loved swimming. Being in the water. She adored floating along with a snorkel. Enjoying the silence and the buoyancy. Each spring, when she dove back into a municipal pool for the first swim of the year, she felt her body in a different way, happy with its sudden weightlessness. The water supporting her was strange and calming. She swam to forget the way some people read to forget. Or to remember.

After her aqua-fitness class, on December 8, she had returned to the apartment in Jersey City and said as she took off her hat, "I do believe I'm happy." Her hair was damp. I don't know if she was nervous, but she was most definitely troubled.

I had kissed the hollow between her clavicle and her neck and inhaled. The scent of shampoo and chlorine.

She also loved cola-flavoured Chupa Chups lollipops. "You can't find them in America."

"Everyone wants to be right. No one is wrong, once a few criteria are met: the untruth and the hope. And no woman has ever been pope. What are they so afraid of? They all came out of a vagina." I didn't want to answer because the answer would just be discouraging.

154

She had a big, round belly. We made love lying on our sides. Or on all fours like mammals. She always clenched the blanket in her fists. Her belly scared me. An architecture. Someone else was growing in there. A bit of me. Women push us toward the vortex between two buildings. Now and later.

She had kept her bra on. Some nights, it stayed in place and others, it disappeared. Never did understand why. Afterward, she'd said, "A mirror can increase the value of something and then, the next time, take it away." She was paraphrasing Italo Calvino in *Invisible Cities*. I am more and more convinced that she knew how our story would end. If not, her death would be meaningless.

"I remember the day I learned to tie my shoelaces." She was six years old. Her mother had dressed her in white wool tights that made her legs itch. First day of school. Pink girls' Converse running shoes. The thrill of new clothes just barely neutralized the nervousness.

The simple knot first, then the two ends. You go around the finger and then the two hands pinch the loops as you pull one away from the other to form the final two, which you tighten on both sides to make them symmetrical. "Some moments are worth more than others."

Moments like when we kissed for the first time. I would like them to be recorded in our story like the loops of your shoelaces. There was a table, a bench seat. And this extraordinary urge to put my lips on yours so that the world could continue to exist at that precise moment. I felt your body. Its benediction. The one that says yes to this space. An ambiguous tunnel. The directed intention.

The only one possible. Like a goal scored in overtime. Unequivocal. A ring on the third finger of each hand. Your silver chain with the olivewood cross. On the little finger of your left hand, a third ring, delicate and dull, made of worn white gold, your mother's. Your butterfly earrings. "The spiritual death of butterflies," you had written, which had no clear connection to the shopping list that was held to the refrigerator's magnetic door by a yellow plastic butterfly. Red vintage shoes from the 1980s inherited from your grandmother, with a strap over the ankle; a red-and-gold dress hemmed just above the knee, with a horseshoe motif; your hair pulled up into a chignon; your eyes made up just enough to forget the makeup and glistening lips that hoped to be kissed. Red, too. It was 23° Celsius. You told me that you loved me four times.

We will live outside the realm of worries and fear: "Never underestimate a man in love."

I trembled the first time I said "I love you." The second time, I was surprised. The third, I had doubts and the fourth, I believed in it. Everything is fine. I feel good. Especially when I know that I am the last man standing. Once again. "I will not break my vows, I promise."

DECEMBER 16.
BRANKA:
"YOU KNOW THAT

in the original Brothers Grimm story, Cinderella's step-sisters cut off their toes so that they could put on the shoe. Hoping to fool the Prince so that he would decide to marry one of them. They even got into the coach with him to show him that the shoe fit. And just as the Prince was preparing to accept what they said, a little bird whispered to him that the carriage was covered in blood." And so he understood the horror and the lie.

"Why did Disney change the story? He lied to us, hoping to spare us something he thought was repugnant." You have to be wary of lies, but maybe especially of omissions. Especially the hypocritical ones that are meant to improve the race. Even lying to yourself, for your own good. Indulgences.

"They cut off their toes? Don't you think that's an important part of the story?" she'd barked, pretending to be angry but with a smile on her face. I had nodded in agreement.

"My favourite movies are the ones where the hero dies before the end, but preferably right at the beginning. That way, there's less bullshit."

I'M
SURE STAN
HAD WONDERED

what it would be like to die. Exactly what happens when the functions of the blood can no longer nourish the mind? Aside from the suffocation of the flesh, will the moment that follows the last second of life be the way they say it is? Like in those accounts of dead people coming back to life that we find so delightful. Is it possible that everything simply shuts off? That the light at the end of the tunnel is visible only when we're expelled from the belly of a woman.

Stan had felt both the buoyancy of happiness and the weight of the shackles he wore. He had atoned. It's a privilege unique to the dead. A knowledge that I will put off acquiring for several years yet. Running from it.

Branka gained this knowledge, too. At the same moment. The two individuals whose centres I will come the closest to. In a single instant. Somewhere between the sidewalk in an American city and an orbit around the Earth.

I'M
WALKING
BY MYSELF.

It is almost four o'clock in the afternoon. It's dark. Soon it will have been one full day. It seems that a memory, whether of a sorrowful or happy thing, lasts fourteen days. After that, all the emotions are reduced by more than half. That will take me to sometime around the Feast of the Epiphany. In the hope that all of this is true. Provided that there's a star out that night. Or coloured dust in the night to show me the way.

It snowed in Brooklyn today. Snowflakes that muffle sounds. Less noise from horns, sirens and trucks. We often wonder how significant moments become idealized. They are either imposed with violence or they are absorbed like a drop of water.

"When Branka died." It doesn't explain anything, for once, but it makes the statement indispensable. For seconds as for millennia. I don't know if I loved this woman. I believe I did. I miss her. It's not the discomfort of absence that hurts but a breach in the desire. You can build from there. Some days, the attraction was fusional. There was no salvation apart from her. Even physically. I would have stayed inside her for centuries. Excited by the simple and rare feeling of being more alive like that. "How are you going to prove to me that He doesn't exist?"

We would have a son. A normal perpetuation that had already been arranged. A reversal of the history of Judea. Our meeting at Easter. Your death at Christmas. And voilà , you would have had time to say as you fell, "God does not exist."

159

So now I know it's true. He couldn't have invented our history. There are no connections. Except those that you want. There's not even absurdity. Events. Directed. Your body must be at the morgue. Cold and stiff. A hole in the back of your head and a ghastly opening under your nostril. It remains a mystery. Aside from the liveliness of bodies, I understand even less. It is through immobility that everything should be proven, not through forward progress. It's a failure. In the beginning, there was no movement at all.

You had given me a little round tinplate witch on Halloween and I took it back to Montreal and hung it in the bathroom of my apartment on Jeanne-Mance. It's still there. That's the beauty of inanimate objects: they never die. They remain immobile and continue to exist. Like a miracle. And it is through them that we attach ourselves with invisible wires to other things – things that have the misfortune of being able to die. The need for relics. I felt good on the Brooklyn Bridge last night, watching the water flow.

You liked Calder's mobiles because they have the simplicity essential of their identity. Nothing more, nothing less. Common shapes, suspended, unpretentious. Almost like that man in space. A story without embellishment. Since we know that life cannot be eradicated, it's life's consciousness that we should pay attention to. "Consider for a moment that we are nothing but the sum of a few coincidences, some cells and biology: that makes us accountable for our actions, our gestures and our choices. But if we are merely the will of another or the result of a simple blunder that exists until man is extinct, we are blameless." The Last Judgment would punish every man who had committed a perfect crime.

When love makes us lose all sense of reason, it's called a crime of passion and this can be explained to the Court. But what do we call it when love leads us to put an end to life? Who has the authority to judge that? Nothing and no one could judge me.

She had also given me a little box for Christmas, yesterday, just before we went out. She had insisted that I keep it with me. "Only open it if you don't keep your promise," she said. A little rectangle the size of a credit card but a little thicker. Wrapped with red paper that had Santa heads printed all over it. Shiny green ribbon. I kept the promise. The box is still in the left pocket of my coat. In the right, I have my keys, my phone and some lozenges. In the left are the important things: bank book, money, business cards. And this little Christmas present that Branka had pressed upon me.

I remember that she also loved burnt marshmallows and the noise a fire makes. That she blinked frequently when she looked at me.

That she always twisted a lock of hair when we talked about the next day.

She was a little shorter than I am. She had to look up every time she spoke to me. It was side by side, on the crumpled sheets, that we might have been the same height. "I don't trust ideas," she had said. "Too many ideals, which makes me forget the present and makes me sad." Pause.

As she often did in the morning, she had gotten up and put on one of my shirts. She had smiled as she looked at herself in the mirror. "I buttoned myself all crooked."

Walking away, her back to me, she'd said, "Our actions are worth a thousand times more than the billions of stories that recount our lives." Then she sat on the toilet without closing the bathroom door. I'll miss that, too.

We have the duty to lie to ourselves. I will skirt around the issue, in the aftermath of your death, Branka. Otherwise it's too hard. The truth is a gap. Stan could not handle it any longer. We are not orbits. We never were. We are spirals.

SARAH
AND
HENRY
WILL SPEND

the rest of their lives together. Because they choose to. In the only freedom that has not been restricted. They chose to love each other and walk the road as two. They could have been three, four, five. Anniversaries were invented to measure our lives. To combat the expiration date. Seven or eight decades that serve as a shield.

Will they ever again articulate, to another stranger like me, the emptiness that unites and divides them? Sarah. His traces still vivid between her legs, forty years later. It's in the head that this does not coagulate. She would have so liked to strike back at life. To pay it back in coin. Seek compensation through vengeance. Smiling, victorious and mute, in the face of the wrongdoer. Believing in the triumph of nature. That a true justice exists. At the bottom of a trench, on a hospital bed, across the flood of tears, a Sunday with the family, explaining famine to children whose mouths are full, so that the discrepancies fall silent, so that the suffering ceases to overwhelm, so that questions are resolved and the emptiness no longer swallows us whole.

The most hurtful part of a miscarriage is the shattering of hope. Other months, we have none; it's just a matter of sanitary napkins.

DECEMBER 19.
IT WAS SNOWING
IN
NEW YORK.

Fifth Avenue. Macy's, Barneys, Cinderella Garbage D. I watched her touch the clothes with her right hand. I played a secondary role. Passersby smiled when they noticed her huge belly under her open coat. An inexplicable happiness? Compassion? Empathy? Or the silent satisfaction that someone else was going to ensure the future of the race? She had asked if I would think it weird if he were born on the 25th. "Not really," I'd answered, since this date was no more than a historical consensus. "Do you know of any others?" she'd said, without turning toward me but continuing to study the price tag on a black-and-white dress. She was as happy in a high-fashion boutique as she was in a second-hand shop.

Her silence was also a consensus. The opposite of the many words we say over and over to ourselves, fearing days that seem too much like all the others.

"All my atheistic prayers, from the time I was twelve, were prayers I said to myself, but ever since he started moving, I also pray to him from time to time." She put her hand, the same one that had held the price tag a moment ago, on top of her belly, just under her breasts.

She was wearing my Yankees hat. I had pulled down the collar of her coat, her scarf and the edge of her blouse. I lifted her hair and put my lips to the red-hot nape of her neck. One, two, three seconds. I think she closed her eyes. Her scent. For an instant. Don't worry, Branka, everything's fine. Do you believe that this is tenderness? "I'm asking you the question." Tenderness is important, right? Maybe that's what saves us from our most grievous hours, so different from all the rest and wearing us to the bone. A perfect reconciliation. She would think about it and would talk to me about it later. The 24th.

Because with a wave of the hand, we can almost touch euphoria. Sustained by desire, we can easily stop the sands of time. Suspended – with fists powerfully clenched around the rope in our hands – over the void.

I don't regret a thing. I didn't regret anything before now. A kiss. An eyelid that fluttered against mine, your leg on my leg under a blanket, the back of my hand on your back. These things, I will miss.

BETWEEN STAN AND ME, BRANKA LEFT PARIS AND FOLLOWED

her mother to America. Three years to rebuild herself. Columbia University, PhD in Art History. Trying to understand, through daily acts and the American dream, all that this had to offer. Land of hope and redemption. Three years of studying, Starbucks caffe lattes, and a job as a waitress in a bistro where the woman who ran the place asked her to greet the clients in French on nights and weekends. She worked to pay for school. Also to buy books after borrowing hundreds from the public library. "It knows how to leave traces," she had said one night when we were discussing technology. "Here, success is more believable when it goes through failure first." And all those hours she had spent at the Baptist church on Montgomery, at the corner of the street where her government-subsidized apartment was located, trying to understand, with apparent piety, what billions of men, women and children could possibly find comforting in an existence greater than the self. She failed to understand. Even through her efforts to forgive, to love and to be uplifted, she could not comprehend why people had sought to abdicate their responsibility as humans by inventing a god. Centuries of belief had been rammed down her throat, telling her that she had to yield to a moral authority designed like a movie. Her favourite film was *A Clockwork Orange*. Because Alex was all of us, rolled into one.

"It would be so lovely if America would die of sepsis."

She also found consolation in flowers. Especially little ones. "I don't know why," she said. "Don't ask me to make sense when there is none, trying to explain every little thing is a mistake. There are things that can't be justified, but that's okay. Because it will keep us from thinking that everything that exists is related to a cause and an effect." Even if it's a skyscraper or a cliff. "Because in both cases, between the exhilaration of the vortex and the real fear of falling, it's the space down below that motivates us." And when it's love?

I REMEMBER
DECEMBER 8.

That morning, she came back, happy, after her aqua-fit class.

"Today, it's the year 1430 in the Muslim calendar and the year 5770 in the Jewish calendar," she'd said. Early evening. I was watching TV. A football game and Christmas advertisements. Branka was kneading bread dough, coating her hands with canola oil every few minutes. "My grandmother's recipe." She wore black jeans, unbuttoned. Bare feet in ballerina flats. A white Gap camisole that was about to explode over her swollen belly. Her hair pulled into a bun and held by a butterfly-shaped clip. "Did you know that canola doesn't exist?" Jutting her chin toward the plastic bottle, she had continued before I could respond: "It's rapeseed oil, but one day someone somewhere assumed – you understand that, an assumption? – well, someone assumed that the word 'rapeseed' wasn't very marketable, so they replaced it with the name of a company: Canola, for Canadian Oil Company, because in Canada, on the Prairies, that's where you find endless fields of the magnificent rapeseed!" She wasn't even being cynical.

That was the moment when I understood what she was trying to say. In retrospect. When we know how to look – and sometimes we do so unintentionally – there are places from which we will not escape. I would have chosen a moment that was serious, sombre and unnamed. This is what happens when you believe too deeply in the stories we've heard since we were very young.

The unspeakable act she was asking of me.

WHEN I LEFT
SARAH AND HENRY'S,

it was dark outside. Twenty-four hours. I said goodbye with great sincerity. They allowed me to leave as I had come in. Simply. Twenty-four hours out of a life. I will disappear from theirs. I think they said "Farewell" when I walked out, just before the door closed behind me. I'm not sure that I heard it. Like yesterday, on the bridge over the East River. I don't remember if the gun made a noise when it hit the water.

ON THE SIDEWALK
ON THE CORNER

of Meserole and Leonard in Brooklyn.

The snow has stopped falling. Soon it will be night again. The evening of December 25th. There are wreaths of multi-coloured lights winking in the windows. The city is abnormally calm, as if the population was respecting a ceasefire. There is a fire hydrant. Towing signs, a surveillance camera, an American flag, garbage bags. I sit down. The same fire hydrant I sat near last night.

In the summer, in Saint-François-de-Sales, we always gathered around the village sports centre's fire hydrant, in the parking lot across from the library. Do you really have to dowse burning books with water?

When we were sixteen, Stan and I had summer jobs working for the town's municipal service. We drove a pick-up, and with a huge wrench in hand, we drained the aqueducts and the fire system, as other students had done before us each spring. It would be nice if we could drain ourselves of the empty air that weakens us.

"Stan?" I guess he doesn't hear me. It must be cold up in space. "Is it going better now?" You must be light already. You're smiling. Have you finally managed to weigh yourself down? They're talking about you a lot down here.

"Time also rotates around a centre, the hour hand, then the minute hand, we just have to do the same," she had said as I fell asleep. I think it was the time she got pregnant. "Let's not be fooled by the end." She was quoting Dorothy Parker from memory as she pulled the sheet around her.

THERE WAS THE SOUND
OF THE CLOCK

in the kitchen.

"Of all the actions we take, it's the vow that requires the most effort and courage," she had said after talking about tenderness, just before she was killed. It's in this vow that I understood that life fades away. Not just your own, but all those that count.

"I love the sound the second hand makes," she had said.

A WIND
FROM THE EAST
CHILLS THE
DAMP AIR

of an American ocean, one Christmas Day. Our limits are often those of our bodies. There are billions of complicated things that I understand. And a few other simple things that completely escape me. Life made me lucky. Since the beginning, we have invented different kinds of magic to explain what we cannot understand. No longer having to turn in place. Refusing the centrifuging lies. Having a centre like all galaxies do. Even at the price of death. Or accepting responsibility for the lie, committing an act.

Against nature.

Setting the meter back to zero.

I will be the only forward movement.

"Will we make it all the way to the vow before the beauty of the world completely disappears?" Branka. Again. "We should never have to adapt ourselves to something just because we're lovers."

One last time.

I began to walk again. I could hear Christmas carols coming from behind closed doors. Adults who accept and children who are happy. A holiday that was once religious. From the past.

DECEMBER 24TH.
YESTERDAY
IN JERSEY CITY.
4:51 P.M.

The limitation of her body. She had talked to me of tender-ness, saying, "Trust only those who doubt," as she lifted the strands of her hair and held them above her ears with bobby pins. She was wearing a short sleeveless dress made of black-and-white terrycloth, pale leather boots and black leggings. It was the first time I'd seen her in that dress. It would be Christmas that evening. "I've had it for ten years, I've waited a long time. This is the first time I'm wearing it." Then she had kissed my cheek and smiled.

Marc Séguin divides his time between his home in Montreal
and his Brooklyn, New York, studio. He has exhibited his art
(the painting details that appear on these covers are his works)
at the most prestigious contemporary exhibitions and fairs,
including those held in Venice, Basel, New York and Miami.
Poacher's Faith was his first novel, *Hollywood* his second;
both in translation with Exile Editions.